"Let Me... It's Been So ̲̲̲̲̲, ̲̲̲̲̲̲̲."

Small explosions of delight flared through her when the rough skin of his fingers moved against the smooth flesh at her neckline, then downward, edging her passion beyond reason, until a single word broke the spell. *Princess.* The link to the past.

"No!" she cried urgently, straining back against his hands, which continued to hold her. "No! I can't do that!" She trembled as the extent of her near-folly hit her.

"Can't?" he challenged hoarsely.

"Won't," she amended in a whisper, slowly, very slowly regaining her composure. Eleven years ago she hadn't refused him. But things were different now. . . . And so was she.

BILLIE DOUGLASS

enjoys writing romances and confesses that her "family, friends, and imagination" influence what ultimately comes from her typewriter. She spends hours at the library researching ("backseat traveling") new and interesting locations. Ms. Douglass lives in Massachusetts with her husband and three sons.

Dear Reader:

Silhouette has always tried to give you exactly what you want. When you asked for increased realism, deeper characterization and greater length, we brought you Silhouette Special Editions. When you asked for increased sensuality, we brought you Silhouette Desire. Now you ask for books with the length and depth of Special Editions, the sensuality of Desire, but with something else besides, something that no one else offers. Now we bring you SILHOUETTE INTIMATE MOMENTS, true romance novels, longer than the usual, with all the depth that length requires. More sensuous than the usual, with characters whose maturity matches that sensuality. Books with the ingredient no one else has tapped: excitement.

There is an electricity between two people in love that makes everything they do magic, larger than life—and this is what we bring you in SILHOUETTE INTIMATE MOMENTS. Look for them this May, wherever you buy books.

These books are for the woman who wants more than she has ever had before. These books are for you. As always, we look forward to your comments and suggestions. You can write to me at the address below:

Karen Solem
Editor-in-Chief
Silhouette Books
P.O. Box 769
New York, N.Y. 10019

BILLIE DOUGLASS
Flip Side Of Yesterday

Silhouette Desire

Published by Silhouette Books New York

America's Publisher of Contemporary Romance

Other Silhouette Books by Billie Douglass

Search for a New Dawn
A Time for Love
Knightly Love
Sweet Serenity
Fast Courting

 SILHOUETTE BOOKS, a Simon & Schuster Division of
GULF & WESTERN CORPORATION
1230 Avenue of the Americas, New York, N.Y. 10020

ISBN: 0-671-45838-8

First Silhouette Books printing April, 1983

10 9 8 7 6 5 4 3 2 1

America's Publisher of Contemporary Romance

Printed in the U.S.A.

For true freedom of the spirit

Flip Side
Of Yesterday

1

The evening breeze was gentle, softly whispering her name as the long-legged vision in white wisked across the dusky lawn, her dark hair streaming behind her, and ran lithely up the broad stone steps.

"Chl . . . ooo . . . eeeee. . . . Chloe! There you are! I was beginning to worry!" A man stepped from beneath the deep brick overhang and fell into easy step beside her as they passed through a large oak door into the high school and headed down a long corridor.

"I'm sorry, Howard." Her voice was as smooth and forthright as the sweet zephyr outside. "I had intended to be on the road by four, but there was a conspiracy against me! First the phone . . . then my car!"

"Anything major—with either?" he asked.

She shook her head, setting fine black silk to swirl about her shoulders. "No. On both counts. But I didn't clear Little Compton until five, and by that time the rush-hour traffic was ghastly! I drove as quickly as I could." Her pink-glossed lips thinned into a frown. "I hope I haven't messed things up."

"No problem." Her companion quickly eased her fear. "The meeting was called for seven thirty. You're only five minutes late. It's given the crowd a chance to settle down." He guided her around a corner with a light hand at her elbow, losing no time as they reached a staircase and began the climb.

At the first landing Chloe's thoughts rushed ahead. "Is the turnout good?" Her smoky gaze probed the man beside her. Howard Wolschinski was the state senator who had first sought her services. Through three previous meetings they had established a fine working relationship.

His grin bore its share of sheepishness. "I only wish we did half as well at political rallies. This is a welcome change from apathy. The auditorium is packed! There must be several hundred people in there."

A shapely brow arched to register Chloe's surprise and pleasure. "Several hundred . . . Not bad for a county meeting—even in New Hampshire!" She smiled, lowering her voice dramatically. "But which *side* are they on? Are they *for* us or *agin'* us?"

Her note of humor drifted unanswered into the stale schoolhouse air as she was ushered into the meeting hall, led directly onto the stage, and shown a seat. Howard took his by her side. As though on cue, the crowd silenced and the moderator began.

"Ladies and gentlemen," he said in a voice made flat by its broad New England hum, "on behalf of my friends and"—he cast an encompassing glance backward, then turned a cough into a snicker, which in turn inspired echoes from the audience—"adversaries here on the stage with me, I would like to thank you for coming tonight. It's a rare pleasure to see so many of you gathered together at one time. We realized that the issue of the Rye Beach Resort and Condominium Complex would stir a few of you to action, but we had no idea how many! As a matter of fact, I don't believe we've had a response like this since that talk of a state prison here a while back. . . ."

Just as Chloe asked herself the question, it was answered in a whisper at her ear. "He's Felix Hart— master of ceremonies, town manager, commissioner of public safety, would-be President of the United States."

A spontaneous smile lit her face at her friend's facetious suggestion. Nodding her thanks for the information, she refocused her attention on the speaker.

". . . and they listened to us. Just as they listened to us when they mentioned a hazardous waste disposal center six miles from us. And before that, there was the matter of a state sales tax."

The discourse continued unwaveringly, freeing Chloe for several seconds more. Bending forward, she extricated a notebook from her bag and prepared to make notes on any points the opposition might raise. That opposition sat to her left, occupying the two chairs on the far side of the one vacated by the moderator. Her peripheral vision took in the presence of two men, one significantly taller and darker than the other. They would be the state representative in favor of the complex and the owner of the development company, though Chloe knew neither of their names. It was a situation that was about to be remedied, as the moderator's words caught her interest at last.

". . . As for the others of us at your disposal tonight, let me begin at your far left. Howard Wolschinski, our distinguished state senator . . ." He gestured in the proper direction as he spoke. ". . . Chloe MacDaniel, geological consultant and one of the founding partners of Earth Science Education, Inc., out of Little Compton, Rhode Island." Chloe nodded with a brief smile before his hand beckoned toward the unknown on the opposite side of the podium. "Bradbury Huff, your state representative"

—she jotted the name in her notebook—"and finally, the president of the Hansen Corporation, Ross Stephenson . . ." R-O-S-S S-T-E——

Chloe's pen stopped in midstroke, frozen by the tremor that whipped through her slender frame. Ross Stephenson? *Ross Stephenson?* She would never forget that name. Could it be a coincidence? Instinct drew her widened gaze to the fourth member of the panel. He was the taller of the two, the darker. How could she tell? This man was dressed in impeccable fashion, groomed likewise. The Ross she had known had been bearded and worn faded jeans, high boots, and a peasant shirt of Indian cotton. How *could* she tell?

His eyes. They were the same. So many years ago their amber intensity had cut through all pretense, capturing her at first glance. Now their acuity was no less. As the rest of existence hung in suspension he held her gaze with unquestionable awareness, reflecting her own sense of shock, of remembrance, of fleeting pain, before she wrenched her eyes away and lowered them defensively to her paper. P-H-E-N-S-O-N. Done. *It was Ross!* Eleven years later.

"Are you all right, Chloe?" Howard whispered softly, having somehow sensed her distress.

For an instant she contemplated lying. But today's Chloe was too honest for that. She turned toward Howard in hopes of hiding the worst of her shakiness from the man at the far side of the stage. "I knew him—Ross—a long time ago," she whispered. "I never expected to see him here." Or *again*, for that matter, she added silently, struggling to keep her thoughts from racing back in time.

"He shakes you up?"

Her smile was rueful. "He shakes me up."

"Will you be able to go on and speak?"

Howard's concern brought her back to the present. "Oh, I'll be fine . . . once we get going." She looked toward Felix Hart, whose gesticulations had, if anything, grown more active.

"He's been sidetracked on the background of your pal. Listen."

Chloe had no choice.

"As many of you know," Felix drawled with a distinct sense of self-importance, "Mr. Stephenson has been behind the building of two successful mall complexes here in the Granite State. His company has left its mark from coast to coast in factories, libraries, educational facilities, and office buildings. The reputation of the Hansen Corporation precedes him here. It is with great honor that I present to you, for an explanation of his plans and hopes for the Rye Beach Complex, Mr. Ross Stephenson."

The hammering of Chloe's heart was joined by the applause of the throng before her, giving her the momentary courage to dart a second glance at Ross. Again he caught her gaze; again he held it. The hammering halted in that instant. She held her breath as memories of yesterday gathered and surged, spreading a slow pallor beneath the ivory sheen of her skin. Then, with a nearly imperceptible nod, he pushed himself from his chair in one fluid movement, approached the dais, and turned his attention forward.

"Whew," came the whispering voice at her ear. "That was quite some greeting." Crimson replaced her pallor as Chloe misinterpreted Howard's observation, then faded slowly as his meaning sank in. "Felix introduced him as though he were a visiting dignitary rather than the man whose blueprints we intend to tear apart!"

Chloe's low-murmured "Please keep reminding me" brought a chuckle from the senator. Then they both settled back to listen to Ross Stephenson's presentation.

For Chloe, it was an awesome challenge. Her eyes were trained on the tall figure standing straight and confident before the microphone. She couldn't help but admire the breadth of his shoulders and the slow tapering of his frame toward narrow hips and long, lean legs. And, to her chagrin, she couldn't help but remember the skin beneath, firm and drawn taut over the muscles of shoulder, chest, and arms, its dark matting of manly hair a warm cushion for her head, an enticing playground for her fingertips.

She forced her fingers to work now, making notes on the words that her ears barely heard, that her mind surely could not assimilate at this emotion-laden moment. With the utmost effort she forced herself to concentrate, jotting down thoughts with increasing rapidity as she realized that only her full involvement with the issue of the evening would free her from the past.

But was it the past that brought her head up again, that funneled her gaze on Ross's commanding presence? Was it the past that inspired her interest in that head of dark hair, full but well trimmed, and combed into as much submission as its thickness would permit? *Then* it had been longer and fuller, if possible, and complemented by the beard that had stretched from ear to ear. *Then* it had given him the aura of a bear—large, overpowering, dominant, yet cuddly. Now there was a refinement about him, a control in his stance, a purposefulness in his approach, as he conveyed competency and intelligence to his audience.

Chloe closed her eyes for a moment of chasing memories. When she opened them she sought the audience's reaction to Ross. They were listening, enrapt, some nodding, others shaking their heads, all measuring his words with the same sense of interest that had brought them out on this mild September evening.

"The benefit to your community would be manifold." His deep voice flowed through the mike, filling the hall with its resonance. "We are proposing to use a parcel of land that is presently underused. We will build a resort to draw a wealth of interest in and patronage of local businesses. Food outlets, entertainment houses, restaurants, real estate establishments—all stand to gain from the Rye Beach Complex." Chloe listened, finding herself swayed by his persuasive lilt. "The condominium complex will bring untold tax revenue both to state and local purses. We have no doubt that, given the easy access to this area by the federal highway system, the condominium units will be in high demand year round." Was this the same Ross who had once defied the establishment and chosen to live on a communal farm in Kentucky? Chloe fought to reconcile the image of that free-spirited Ross with this entrepreneurial one; it was nearly impossible. The best she could do was hone in on this present figure as she might a total stranger against whom she must argue in a very, very short time.

Howard nudged her lightly. "He's a powerful speaker. What do you think? Will he have them on his side before we even present ours?"

He had leaned close to whisper to her. She was able to answer him without taking her eyes from Ross.

"No." She took the optimistic tack. "These people will be pretty open. I've worked often with groups of shoreline residents. They feel very strongly about their finest resource: the land. My appeal will be for the preservation of that very resource."

"You're a powerful speaker yourself, Chloe. Remember, I heard you before that group on Martha's Vineyard when you were discussing natural erosion patterns. You had them eating out of the palm of your hand."

Chloe smiled, appreciating the encouragement. "Many of the issues are the same here. Let's hope they buy it as well!"

Their whispering tapered off as Ross finished his formal presentation, then opened the floor for questions. A podium and microphone had been set up in the central aisle of the auditorium; one by one, those residents who wished came forward. Most asked about specifics, all of which Chloe noted on her pad: the price range of the condominiums and the subsequent tax revenue; the time projection for the erection of the units; the capacity of the resort complex; and a listing of its self-contained facilities. At length, Felix Hart stood and joined Ross at center stage.

"I'm afraid that we've got to move on now," he apologized, making a point of eyeing the large clock that rested on the front face of the balcony. "There is still another side to hear and consider." He turned to Ross. "Thank you, Mr. Stephenson. You've been very direct and a great help. Perhaps there will be more time for questions later."

Chloe watched with growing excitement as Ross returned to his seat. For the moment she was protected from his spell by the anticipation of her own presentation. It was always like this when she spoke, which was often. Though she loved the scientific end of her job—the sample-taking and analysis, the computer work, the intricate calculations of ground composition, weather-related components, time predictions—she found the dissemination of her findings to be its most exhilarating facet.

Felix Hart's introduction broke through her bubble of expectancy. "I have the delightful task now of introducing to you Ms. Chloe MacDaniel." Chloe felt a myriad of eyes turn to her, not the least curious of which were from her far left. "Ms. MacDaniel has been retained by the county to study our coast with an eye toward the environmental impact of the Rye Beach Resort and Condominium Complex as the Hansen Corporation proposes it. She has already spent a good deal of time on the project. So, without further ado, I present to you Ms. MacDaniel."

After lifting a neat folder from the floor beneath her chair, Chloe stood to her full five-foot-eight-inch height and smoothly approached the podium. Her appearance was, as always, understated. Yet just as nothing could hide the beauty of the rugged coastline she championed, nothing could camouflage her own natural beauty. The curiosity of the crowd yielded to a soft murmur of appreciation as she stepped forward. Tall and willowy, dark haired and light complected, she was the image of grace. Her dress was of a soft and simple white eyelet fabric, lined through the bodice and skirt, the sleeves hanging free and loose to her elbows. A wide sash of contrasting aqua enhanced both the slimness of her waist and the beauty of her coloring.

She kept her sights forward, denying the eyes behind her, eyes that recalled her as a sophisticated eighteen-year-old, a girl on the verge of womanhood, on the verge . . . and beyond. Those amber eyes surveyed her in profile, remembering the Chloe of New Orleans society, dressed in designer wear, coiffed and made up to perfection. She had been a striking flower then, but she had matured into a magnificent jewel, shedding all superficiality in the process.

"Thank you, Mr. Hart"—her voice was steady and well modulated—"for the kind introduction. Let me say how pleased I was to have been approached by your representatives last spring. Not only do I have obvious professional interests in your coastline, but I have a definite emotional involvement with the entire New England coast. In keeping with this, I must begin by saying that I am *not* opposed to the building of the Rye Beach Resort and Condominium Complex *per se*. What Mr. Stephenson has outlined for you sounds like a project that could benefit you all." To her dismay the mention of his name brought a momentary quaver to her voice. Pouring her concentration into the coming arguments, she went on more steadily. "What I question, however, is the ecological wisdom of the plan as it stands. Although the thought of a beachfront condominium is appealing to the romantic in us all, this is *not* an environmentally wise plan."

As she proceeded to explain the core results of her tests, she found herself totally enmeshed in her work and mercifully oblivious to the keen eyes that scrutinized her from behind. Her genuine concern had to hit its mark.

"In terms of storm surge alone, the Hansen proposal is risky," she argued gently, pointing to the carefully calculated figures now projected on a slide screen. "Once every six or seven years you folks get a storm strong enough to do significant damage to any structures built that close to the beach. If the entire complex were moved back an additional two hundred feet, the risk would be lessened."

Again she explained her theory in detail, venturing into statistics where applicable. By the time she had finished and opened herself to questions, she felt that her arguments had been well received. As had been the case with Ross, the questions dealt with details, some relevant, others less so. In each case she responded with patience and care, exhibiting her concern for the environment throughout. Howard greeted her with delight when she finally returned to her seat.

"Great presentation, Chloe!" he exclaimed. "You did a fantastic job!"

Chloe smiled modestly, almost shyly. "Thanks. I only hope I've accomplished our objective. What happens now?"

"Now," he intoned with mock solemnity, "you endure brief speeches by Brad and myself. Try to stay awake."

She forced an of-course-I-will chuckle, but her thoughts, now that her major responsibility of the evening was over, had already begun to wander. While Felix introduced Bradbury Huff, she glanced sideways at Ross. Folded comfortably into his seat, he appeared to be listening intently to his advocate, the state representative. Chloe took the opportunity to study him freely.

The years had been kind to him. While his dark brown hair had a touch of gray at the sideburns, it was thick and vital, falling onto his forehead with an air of casual class. She had never seen his jaw before, covered as it had been then by a beard. Its strength was evident in the chiseled line from ear to chin, the latter tightening slightly as he concentrated. There were faint crow's-feet at the corners of his eyes, etched into his light tan as proof of laughter. He appeared to be at the utmost of ease, maddeningly confident of his position and devastatingly handsome to boot.

As though her eye-touch had suddenly grown palpable, he blinked once, then turned his head a fraction, letting his gaze rove further, into collision with hers. At that moment time seemed to stop, then reverse, speeding Chloe back over the years to the first time she'd seen him. It had been a beautiful Thanksgiving night. The moment was as clear to her as if it had been yesterday. She had been with Crystal then; in recollection, a flicker of pain coursed through her. Crystal. How she still missed her sister.

"Chloe?" Howard gently covered her clenched fist with his hand. "Are you still here?" He followed her line of vision, then turned back to her. "You can talk with him later—"

"No!" she interrupted, snapping back to the present, tearing her gaze from Ross's hooded expression. With a grimace of embarrassment, she leaned toward Howard. "I'm sorry. It's just that there are . . . memories. . . ."

"There must be," he noted softly. "And from the looks of you, they're pretty painful."

Her answering whisper was slow. "Not all . . ."

"Well, whatever, you're white as a sheet. Can I get you some water or something?"

"No, thanks. I'm fine." At his quirked brow she added, "Really!" before looking toward the podium. "Is Huff almost done?"

"I believe so. I'm next. Take notes for me, will you?" he kidded her softly. "I have a tendency to forget what I say from one minute to the next."

"Baloney!" she chided with a chuckle, feeling better as Howard worked his politician's magic on her.

"Hmmm, I could use some of that, too. Supper was very early. It's nearly ten."

If his supper had been early, at least it was more than *she* had had. *"Ten?"* she whispered back in astonishment. "How much longer do you think this will last?" Brad Huff appeared to be droning on and on, and there was still the return trip to Little Compton to be made this night.

Howard shook his head. "I have no idea. I've got to be out of here by ten thirty to make it to Manchester in time for the eleven o'clock news. They're doing a live interview. I certainly hope good old Brad speeds it up."

His hope was realized. As Chloe sat back, the long-winded state representative transferred the podium to "my illustrious colleague in the New Hampshire state government." Howard took the reins.

Chloe did take notes, for it was the one way she could keep her thoughts in the present, her eyes from that compelling figure of a man so near yet years away. So much had happened since that night. . . .

When Howard finished delivering what Chloe thought was a poignant plea for the preservation of the coast, the crowd, as though suddenly tired of restraint, came alive with questions and comments. Their thoughts were of a more general—and more emotional— nature than before. Their interest centered around the two legislators. How would increased tax revenues be used to benefit local residents? Who would pay for the added police and fire coverage that would be necessary, considering the proportions of the Rye Beach proposal?

It was closer to ten forty before Howard was allowed to drag himself from the microphone. "Thanks again for everything, Chloe." He turned to her for a final word. "Do you think you can take over for me for a few minutes longer?"

"Sure thing, Howard—if, that is, I can answer their questions. My field is geology, not politics."

"Don't underestimate yourself." He grinned. "And, Chloe, why don't you change your mind and spend the night? There are any number of nice inns close by. It'll be an awfully long drive back to Rhode Island alone."

Touched by his worry, she tipped her head up confidently. "I'll be fine. Driving relaxes me. And I have plenty of unwinding to do." From the corner of her eye she caught a movement, a sharp reminder of the source of any tension she felt. Determinedly, she ignored the tall figure who approached. "Go on, now, Senator. You'll be late!"

Howard's expression was wry. "I already am. Take care, Chloe." He darted a quick glance up. "And let me know what happens." If his double meaning had been meant as humor, she found none in it. Naturally Howard would want to know her reactions to the evening and the further dialogue he would miss. As to the other . . .

"I think they'd like to ask us several questions." The deep voice and towering figure could only be Ross. Chloe suddenly wished Howard had stayed, if only to serve as a buffer. Now she was on her own.

With a forced smile, she stood. "Fine," was all she was able to murmur, vitally conscious as she was of the presence beside her as she walked to the podium.

Fortune was on her side; the questions from the audience came quickly, demanding her reimmersion into the world of coastal geology. She parried the onslaught with ease, rising to meet the challenge in spite of the odd feeling in the pit of her stomach. It was only when a question was directed toward Ross that she lapsed into active awareness of him once more—the breadth of his shoulders, more obvious now that his jacket was open and pulled back by the left hand in his trouser pocket, his right hand resting on the top of the podium, his fingers, long and straight, tanned and relaxed, capable of such exquisite tenderness. . . .

"I have a question for Ms. MacDaniel." A gruff-looking local was recognized by Felix and addressed himself forcefully to Chloe. Grateful as she was for the bucket of cold water poured onto her silent meanderings, she sensed distinct antagonism in this questioner and tensed. Drawing herself up straighter, she nodded. "Uh-huh?"

"I want to know"—he didn't blink once, merely stared directly at her—"what qualifications you have to serve as a consultant. You look awfully young . . . and awfully pretty. Are you a regular on Wolschinski's payroll?"

The faint sneer in his words and his obvious insinuation sent a murmur of dismay through the audience. It was small solace for the shock Chloe felt. In the past she'd had to defend her qualifications on occasion, but never in the wake of such a crude inference. But poise and professionalism were the order of the moment. As she opened her mouth to speak, however, Ross beat her to the mike.

"I believe," he said as his dark head lowered, "that your question has no relevance—"

For the first time that evening she looked at Ross entirely in the context of the present. "Excuse me for interrupting, Mr. Stephenson"—she leaned toward the mike—"but I *would* like to respond to the gentleman." Her expression brooked no argument. She was determined. Ross straightened and backed off, somewhat bemused as, without pause, she redirected her gaze to the man in the audience.

"First things first, Mr.—"

"—Younger," he supplied, completely dropping the *r* at the end of his name in true New England form.

"—Mr. Younger. I have a bachelor of science in geology from Williams College in Williamstown, Massachusetts, and a master's in geology from Boston College. I spent three years working for ConAm Petroleum, performing geological studies on oil deposits in the Gulf of Mexico. I was then able to co-found Earth Science Education, Inc., the consulting firm that was contacted by Senator Wolschinski to study the pros and cons of the Rye Beach Resort and Condominium Complex." Without pausing for so much as a breath and holding the man's gaze steadily, she ventured boldly on. "I have control over neither my age nor my looks. And I never worked for Senator Wolschinski prior to the day he retained my services for this project." Now she did hesitate, breathing in deeply, angling her head in subtle defiance. "Have you any other questions?"

Again a collective murmur undulated through the crowd. Just as the man shrugged and stepped back, Chloe saw the hand on the podium lift, drawing her attention to Ross's face. She saw a look of astonishment, barely hidden beneath a veneer of outer control. His long fingers absently stroked his jawline as a mélange of perplexity, satisfaction, and respect crossed his features in rapid succession.

It was evidently not only Ross whom she had impressed. Her dark head snapped back as a different voice rose from the audience. "The taxpayers' money has been well spent for a change. Thank you, Ms. Mac-Daniel!"

Buoyed by her victory, Chloe allowed herself to aim a full smile across the ocean of heads as she leaned toward the microphone one final time. "It's been my honor. If my effort here has helped to preserve the natural bounty of your state, then we've all benefited. Thank you."

It was the perfect time to make a gracious, if not

sweeping, exit. With Ross Stephenson still standing to the
side in deference to her captivation of the crowd and that
crowd applauding its very definite appreciation, she
should have quit while she was ahead. Her mistake was
in looking back at Ross.

His smile was devastating, respect having ripened into
warm admiration. Chloe felt her chest tighten as her
memories seized her again, immobilizing her, suspending
her in a matrix of desire and guilt, canceling out the years
that had come between, until there was only yesterday—
yesterday, Ross, Crystal, and the toss of a coin.

It was the spontaneous surge of late-night interest
bringing a share of the audience to the stage that broke
the spell and returned a shaken Chloe to the present.
Perhaps it was fortunate. The further questions posed to
her demanded her concentration, offering her a reprieve.
She stood at one side of the stage, Ross at the other, each
with his own contingent of followers. With each new
question her strength returned, so that when the last of
the locals had bid her good-bye she felt more herself. She
felt more herself, that is, for as long as it took her to scan
the stage and discover that she and Ross were alone.

Startled, she looked out to see the last of the residents
in retreat. Was there no one else? Where had Brad Huff
gone? And Felix Hart? To her dismay, there *was* no one
else. Only Ross—and a world of memories she wanted
desperately to leave behind.

If he shared either her awkwardness or her apprehen-
sion he gave no hint of it. Rather, he smiled at her gently,
looking older and wiser, perhaps, but no less alert.
Already the air was alive with sensual vibration. It had
been that way eleven years ago; it had not changed with
time.

Chloe found herself grappling with a world of inner
demons. The past was something she hadn't dreamt to
resurrect. Her only hope was to make this reunion as
brief as possible.

"How are you, Chloe?" Ross asked, walking over to stand tall before her.

Of necessity she tipped her head up slightly. "Fine, Ross. And you?" It was as though the evening's debate had never taken place, as though they were meeting accidentally on the street.

"Not bad. You're looking . . . very well." His gaze flickered warmly over her. "Quite . . . different." He cleared his throat, unable to hide the ghost of humor hovering at the corners of his lips.

"So are you." Her insides trembled, yet she couldn't help but appreciate and share the taste of humor. "When I last saw you, you were distinctly antiestablishment. This is a switch."

His stance was a casual one, the hand in his pocket not only emphasizing the solid wall of his chest but pulling the fabric of his trousers across his thigh just enough to impress her senses with the muscled strength of seemingly endless legs.

"Not entirely. It's just that now I save my jeans for free-time wear and my boots for cold weather."

So he remembered what he had worn that night, too. "And the peasant shirt?" she heard herself blurt out softly.

He laughed, his eyes crinkling. "The peasant shirt was replaced for a while by a dashiki, but I'm afraid to say that I've become addicted to very ordinary sports shirts and sweaters."

"Conventional," she murmured with a faltering smile, teasing him as much as she dared. It was hard to remain indifferent to this man; Chloe's pulse felt the strain.

"Sadly so," he agreed without a bit of sadness. "And you—you've done quite a turnaround. When I last saw you, your hair was curled, you wore makeup, higher heels, and more daring clothes."

In the instant of recollection Chloe's eyes held enough sadness for them both. Nodding, she chewed on her lower lip, still unable to drag her gaze from Ross. "Time does different things to each of us, I guess."

"It's for the better, Chloe. You look beautiful. Unhappy . . . but beautiful." There was no smugness in his appraisal; it was a simple statement.

His unexpected candor made her balk. Seeing him was painful enough; talking with him could prove to be a total trauma. Since she wasn't wearing a watch, or any jewelry, for that matter, she glanced at the auditorium clock. "My Lord, it's nearly twelve! I've got to run!" Straightening the shoulder strap of her pocketbook and hugging the large folder to her breast, she turned toward the steps. As she had feared he would, Ross walked with her. Under the guise of worry at the lateness of the hour, she quickened her step. He kept stride easily.

"You're not driving back tonight, are you?"

"Uh-huh." Eyes ahead, she missed his frown.

"All the way to . . . ?"

"Little Compton. Uh-huh."

"That's got to be a good two- to three-hour drive. Wouldn't you do better to get an early start in the morning?"

"I've got an early *appointment* in the morning." Her voice sounded breathy. Was it the rush . . . or her companion?

For long moments Ross said nothing. They reached the front door. He held it; she passed through. Both were deep in thought as they crossed the lawn that separated the high school from the parking lot.

"I admire you, Chloe," he said at last, deeply and sincerely. "Your work is very interesting. You obviously enjoy it."

"I do," she agreed softly, relieved to have arrived at her car, awkwardly fishing into her purse for her keys. The sooner she was back to that work, back to the security of her seafront home in Little Compton, the sooner she could forget the past once more. Within moments she had slipped behind the wheel and rolled her window down to let in the refreshingly cool night air. With escape imminent, she grew bolder, looking up at Ross as he bent toward her, his fingers curved over the lowered window. "It was nice seeing you, Ross." How handsome he was, she mused in an instant of guilt-free indulgence. She had been powerfully attracted to him then; now the same tingling burst into being within her.

"You won't change your mind and stay over? I'm staying at the Wayward Sailor, an inn just down the road a bit. I'm sure they'd have another vacancy, since the height of the season is well past. We could talk, over a snack somewhere."

On the one hand, Chloe would have liked nothing better. It occurred to her that she knew nothing about this Ross Stephenson, who was now the president of the Hansen Corporation, save what the moderator this evening had offered in his introduction. Every instinct told her that time spent with Ross would be interesting. Interesting . . . to say the least. On the other hand, it could be downright dangerous and potentially devastating.

"That would be nice, Ross," she answered, in part honestly, "but I do have to get back. I feel wide awake for driving"—Could he guess why? she wondered—"and I'd just as soon put the miles behind me. Besides, I have that appointment."

Ross's shrug of resignation made further excuses unnecessary. In gracious defeat, he stepped back. Chloe put the key into the ignition, pumped the gas pedal once, then turned the key. Nothing happened. "Damn," she muttered to herself. She repeated the sequence a second time. It always worked. Granted, her small blue compact had seen better days, but it had always started for her. Until, she realized as she turned the key a third time, this afternoon. Then there had been this same click. Then she had run back into the house and brought Lee out to help her. Assuming the engine to be flooded, they had waited, and finally met with success. Instinctively, she knew that the engine was not flooded now. Her follow-up curse was aimed half at the engine, half at the company in which she was now stranded.

"Trouble?" He bent low again to look through her window.

"Battery, I think."

"Here." He opened the door to let her out. "Let me try."

With an ease that belied his awesome length, Ross folded himself behind the wheel. The front seat was already back quite a bit to allow for the length of Chloe's own legs. She had to stifle a smile at his grimace, good-natured though it was. Getting in had been fine, it seemed. It was the maneuvering once inside that appeared to present a minor challenge.

Ross ignored it to try his luck with the ignition. Unfortunately, his was no better than Chloe's had been. Time and again he fiddled with the key. Time and again there was nothing more than an impotent clicking sound to reward him for his efforts. With obvious relief—Was it at being freed from the confines of the small car or from another source? Chloe wondered skeptically—he hoisted himself from the driver's seat and confronted the workings beneath the hood. His diagnosis came quickly.

"You're right. It *is* the battery." Straightening, he slammed the hood shut and brushed his palms against one another. "It looks like you'll *have* to stay. I don't see how you'll get someone to come out at this hour."

She reached for her bag. "I have AAA coverage . . ."

"Chloe," he sighed softly. "This isn't a bustling metropolis. By the time—"

"Have you got jumper cables?" Inspiration dawned, to be instantly squelched.

"No. I don't happen to carry them on me." His wryly spoken denial was on the kinder side of sarcasm.

"In your car . . . ?" Her specification fell on unsympathetic ears.

"It's a rental."

"Oh." Her gaze fell to the pavement. It seemed she had little choice. In the dilemma of the moment the past was temporarily forgotten. "I suppose Lee could change that early appointment for me," she murmured quietly, then looked up. "And you think your inn would have a room?"

His gaze held hers steadily. "I'm sure it would."

Not one to belabor a no-win situation, Chloe sighed. "Lead on, Ross. Lead on."

2

Ross led her to a late-model rental car roomy enough for both pairs of long legs to stretch comfortably. Yet Chloe sensed that no space would be large enough to blunt the intensity of feeling that circuited back and forth between them during the short drive to the inn.

"You flew in just for tonight's meeting?" she asked, seeking both to satisfy her curiosity and to relieve a silence made awkward by the knowledge of intimacy once shared.

"That's right," he answered simply, paying close attention to roads now dark and deserted.

"From . . . ?"

"New York."

"You live there?"

"Occasionally."

It was an odd answer. When he failed to elaborate, Chloe sensed his preoccupation. Were his thoughts as disquieting as hers? It seemed unlikely, for he was unaware of the events that had so closely followed their brief liaison. What, then, was distracting him?

Quietly, she tried again. "Have you had to come here often?"

"More often than I'd anticipated. This project has created something of a stir, as you know." If the glance he shot her was at all accusatory, she accepted it as fair under the circumstances and took no offense. She believed firmly in her cause.

"From what Felix Hart implied, you move around quite a bit."

"I always did."

His reference to the past didn't escape her. Then he had been in the Peace Corps on leave for Thanksgiving. There had been an air of excitement about him.

Chloe peered sidelong at his bold profile. Strong, lean, preoccupied. Shrugging, she focused on the view outside her window and tried to ignore the nearly tangible silence. When the Wayward Sailor came into view she breathed a sigh of relief.

Ross turned to her as soon as the car stopped. His features had softened once more and his tone was solicitous. "Why don't you wait here? I'll make the arrangements and find out where we can get a bite to eat. You *are* hungry, aren't you?"

"Uh-huh." She smiled awkwardly. "I haven't had anything since lunch."

"No wonder you're pale!" His hand reached to lightly touch her cheek, but before she could react he had whipped it back himself. He spoke more quickly then. "Stay put. I'll be right back."

She sat quietly for several moments, trying to think of anything but Ross. Then, just when she was on the verge of declaring defeat, his lean form loped easily back down the steps of the charmingly ancient house. "Any luck?" she asked when he reached the car.

"I've got good news . . . and bad news." He seemed to make a habit of leaning down to talk to her through car windows.

Chloe's eyes widened in anticipation. "The good news?" She'd need that first.

"The good news is that you've got the penthouse." He grinned crookedly as Chloe's gaze climbed the inn's facade to its apex, the third story. The attic—if it was clean and had a bed, it would do.

"The penthouse it is. And"— she scrunched up her face, awaiting the blow—"the bad news . . . ?"

"The bad news"—he opened her door with a flourish—"is that no one serves food at this hour. The night manager here has agreed to let us raid his refrigerator, though." He paused, staring down at her for a moment before offering his hand to help her out. "I'm sorry that the service won't be fancy. We'll be on our own." The warning note in his voice jarred her into the realization that he clearly recalled the Chloe of yesteryear. That Chloe had been spoiled, to say the least. She hadn't known how to cook, having had everything done for her for the entire eighteen years of her life. But her life-style had changed drastically since then.

"That's fine, Ross." She stood beside him. "I think we can manage." Oh, yes, she could certainly manage to put together a meal; she was actually quite a fine cook now. But it suddenly occurred to her that she and Ross would be alone . . . again . . . still. Could she manage *that?*

A frown creased her brow as she entered the inn with Ross close by her side. The overnight case he had carried was left at the front desk with the night manager, who cheerfully directed them into the kitchen, a decidedly old room into which every modern convenience had been crammed. Chloe immediately made herself at home. It was only after she had placed a crock of steaming beef stew, put together quickly from leftovers, and a half-loaf of what appeared to be home-baked bread on the table that she realized that *she* had done all the work. Indeed, it had been an escape. Ross had been in and out of the room as she worked, finally settling down on a tall stool by a butcher-block counter to watch.

To her surprise, his presence didn't upset her now as much as it had earlier. Perhaps it had taken time to get over the shock. Whatever, she felt vaguely shy when at last they were ready to eat.

"Ah . . . is there anything else you want?" She skimmed the simple place settings, the two large bowls awaiting stew. "A drink?"

He made no move to help himself. For old times' sake, so the liberated woman within assured her, she indulged him.

"Milk would be fine." He nodded his thanks, then sat back to watch her search for glasses and then fill two. After taking a seat opposite him, Chloe deftly dished out the stew. Only then did her mind replay the shock of the evening. Strangely, one word stuck in her mind. With several mouthfuls of the thick fare warming her stomach, she put her spoon down.

"I'm *not* unhappy," she stated, so softly and unexpectedly that Ross nearly choked. When he looked perplexed, she reminded him of his words. "You thought I looked unhappy. I'm not."

He resumed eating, but more slowly, more thoughtfully. "No, I suppose you're not . . . right now," he finally admitted. "But earlier . . . there was a look in your eyes. It comes and goes. There it is again." His amber gaze sharpened.

Against her will, her thoughts had turned on her, reverting to memories for a fleeting moment. If she could only stay in the present, she would be fine. With a barely perceptible shake of her head, Chloe chased away the ghosts.

"I do love what I'm doing." She channeled the discussion back toward the present and, to her relief, Ross didn't argue.

"Tell me about it, Chloe. How did you get started?"

She shrugged, avoiding his gaze. "You heard the bare outline tonight."

"The bare outline—that's right. Now I'd like to hear more." His pause was pregnant with thoughts unspoken. "Why geology?"

Again her shoulders lifted. "Why not?"

"Because," he countered without hesitation, "it's one of the last fields that a young woman raised in the style of conspicuous consumption would choose."

Her smoky gaze flew to his. "Perhaps that's why I chose it."

"Ah." He smiled, pleased that his tactic had been so successful in drawing her out. "You were rebelling?"

"Not entirely."

"Escaping?"

She looked away. "You're very perceptive. But only half right."

"Go on."

In an unconscious gesture of nervousness, Chloe tucked a long strand of dark hair behind her ear. "It was actually a simultaneous discovery—escape and excitement. At that . . . period of my life, I needed something that was a total change from everything I'd known before. I . . . spent some time in Newport with friends and discovered an attraction to the ocean."

"Solace?" he asked gently.

"If you will. I spent a lot of time on the beach and happened to befriend an old man who felt very strongly about environmental considerations. He affected me deeply." The memory of Hector Wallaby brought a sad smile to her lips.

"He's dead?" Ross read her expression correctly.

"Yes. I miss him. He was, in a sense, the founding father of ESE, Inc.—though he never knew it."

"Were you in college during the time you knew him?"

Jolted from her reverie to the more factual realm of her background, Chloe stiffened. "Ah . . . no. I . . . My freshman year was . . . postponed."

"So you started college late and have *still* managed to do all that you have?"

His obvious appreciation for her dedication bolstered her; it was just what she needed at that moment. "Once I decided to go into geology"—she smiled sheepishly—"I was in a rush."

Ross matched her smile and in so doing sent ripples of appreciation through *her*. Strong male lips framed the whitest of teeth, mesmerizing her for the split second until he moved them.

"You worked for ConAm Petroleum?" He seemed genuinely interested.

"Uh-huh. Are you familiar with them?"

He shook his head. "Only by reputation. I would have thought"—he paused, examining her closely—"that, if environmental concerns were your focus, the oil companies would be your archenemies."

It was no small measure of guilt that brought a flush to her cheeks. The man pulled no punches, *that* was for sure! But his honest expression of his thoughts deserved similar bluntness.

"I needed the money," she announced brazenly, then steeled herself for the response that was sure to come.

Ross's eyes widened, then narrowed, his amber intensity outshining itself. "You needed the money?" Only his half-whispered tone tempered his amazement. "Wait a minute." He frowned. "Have I got something wrong here? I was under the distinct impression that James MacDaniel was—is—one of the wealthiest men in New Orleans."

"He is."

"Then, why . . . ?" His voice trailed off in confusion.

"Among other things, Ross"—she had tensed, defending herself once more—"it was a matter of pride. I wanted to start my own consulting firm and I had no wish to ask my father for money."

He studied the stubborn tilt of her chin and in that instant learned something new. Before him sat a woman who was her own person. But just how deep did her strength run?

"So you sold out to the powers that be for the amount of time it took you to gather the resources to mount a systematic campaign *against* those same powers?" His question carried an indictment that startled Chloe into vehement reaction.

"That's not true! The work I did for the oil companies involved identifying the most likely spots for oil deposits. Wherever possible, environmental considerations were put first." Her eyes had come alive, silver sparks flashing beneath a fringe of charcoal lashes. "And *you're* a fine one to talk about selling out. I had the impression, when I saw you last, that you were against everything the establishment had to offer."

Undaunted by her tirade, Ross leaned back in his chair. "You drew your own conclusions, Chloe. Appearances can often be misleading." His tone was low, his voice steady. His eyes did not release hers for a minute.

It was as though she had been slapped. Stunned, Chloe shot out of her chair, its legs scraping against the wooden floor as it skidded back.

"It was all a charade, then?" she gasped in disbelief. "The clothes, the beard—even the Peace Corps . . ." Whirling away to face her disillusionment, she was oblivious to the look of perplexity that seized Ross's features. He studied her bowed head and tensed back as long as he could bear it, then stood and circled the table to confront her.

"Did it matter so much, Chloe?" he asked softly, trying to understand. When she neither answered nor looked up, he curled his forefinger beneath her chin, lifting it gently. Her eyes were dry, yet bursting with the same pain he had seen earlier that evening. "Did it matter so much?"

Chloe felt a surge of emotion within her, emotion that had lain dormant all those years. Ross was so close to her, the warmth of his body an intoxicant in and of itself. As her gaze touched his features, one by one, she forced herself to speak. "Yes, Ross. It mattered more than you can ever imagine."

"But why?" He cocked his head, puzzled. "The physical attraction we felt for one another had nothing to do with outer trappings. As I recall, we shed our clothes fairly quickly." When Chloe jerked her head away, he brought it back more firmly. "No, Chloe. Don't run away from it. There was something between us that you can't deny. Are you telling me that you made love to an . . . image?" His tone had grown cool with a hurt she hadn't imagined. "Was it an *experiment* for you? Was *I* a tool in your rebellion?" His fingers tightened on her jaw; reflexively, she curled her own around his wrist.

"No! That wasn't it at all!" she lashed back, feeling a hurt herself that he could imagine *that* of her. "All you seem to think of is the *physical act.* Yes, there was a physical attraction. With and *without* clothes. But for me, at least, there was much more involved. There had to be!" Her voice had risen with emotion. "For God's sake, I was a virgin!"

Still unable to fully understand the anguish in her gaze, Ross felt her hurt nonetheless and instantly relaxed his grip. His fingers moved slowly back to her ear, threading through the long strands of her hair with infinite gentleness.

"I know that," he whispered. "I know that." His eyes held the same tenderness they had on that night, when he had first introduced her to the art of love. She was suddenly transported back over time to that night, to a time when the world was hers on a string. Her heart pounded now in her chest, as it had then. Ross's inner wrist, resting against the pulse point at her throat, picked up the beat.

Once more Chloe was in the arms of the most appealing man she had ever known. He was a leader, a freethinker. He was boldly gentle, gently bold. He had confidence without arrogance, success without acclaim. He was a man who didn't mince words. And she felt an instinctive surge of respect for him.

Much of this same appeal had beckoned to her on that night. All else had been unbelievably forgotten but Ross and the unique force bringing them together. It was an unfathomable force, yet all-powerful. Eleven years ago, it had driven the fact of her innocence from her mind. Now it obliterated all remembrance of what had happened so soon after that night to irrevocably change Chloe's life and outlook.

As Ross's large hands framed her face, holding it still, at the mercy of his gaze, she felt a warmth slowly seep through her, awakening senses from hibernation like the honeyed breath of spring. As her cheeks flushed with the heat, her lips parted. She was entranced, as she had been once before.

He moved closer, inches closer, his face lowering as his aura encompassed her. When she closed her eyes it was to savor to the fullest the feather touch of his mouth over hers. It seemed as if she had waited forever to know its sweetness again; its touch was much too brief.

Guilt was now light-years away, beyond a far horizon she hoped never to reach. Pervasive as it had been over the years, it was suddenly irrelevant. Chloe only knew she wanted more of Ross, if only to keep that past safely blotted from mind.

Opening her eyes, she found Ross's own smoldering

above her. He had seen pain earlier that night in the gaze she'd cast him. If it was his kiss that would cause a recurrence, he would not give it. The light in her eyes, though, gave him his answer. There was no pain now save that of desire.

She met his kiss with an eagerness she hadn't known for eleven years. All the power of her femininity, stored up and denied, now surged forth. Ross's lips were firm and masterful in response to her passion, dominating, then submitting, teasing, then yielding. They explored the ripe curve of her mouth with a thoroughness surpassed only when his tongue entered the act to redefine its depth. And Chloe opened herself more with each darting flicker, with each exchange of breath, as a desert to the rain.

She had come alive and was mindlessly aflame with passion. At some point her arms had sought the strong column of his neck and curved beyond, drawing her slender body firmly against his longer, more muscled one. His own hands played havoc with the ultrasensitive skin of her back, caressing every inch from hip to neck with the devastating touch of those long fingers. Caught in the web of desire those fingers spun around her, she was neither able nor willing to move away.

Everything about Ross was utterly male, from the musky scent of his skin to the trim tapering of the hair at the top of his collar, to the lean line of his torso and the corded steel of his thighs. It was, for Chloe, as though she were innocent once more, as though this *was* that first ecstatic night relived. She was intoxicated.

When, with a groan, he released her lips and held her fiercely to him, she understood that fierceness and returned it. It was a statement of primal need, shared by them both, and it couldn't be denied. Ross held something for her that no other man had ever come close to offering. She was driven by instinct closer, closer to him.

At what point soft cries of warning began to intrude on

her whirl of emotion, she didn't know. Was it when his hand caressed her cheek, then fell to curve around her neck for an instant before his fingers trailed back across her throat and fell to her breast? Was it at the moment when his fingers began to trace lazy circles around the fullness he found awaiting him? Was it when she gasped as his palms tantalized the hot point of her nipple, giving it growing life of its own, feeling it swell at his bidding?

She only knew of a slow-born tug between some relic of the past, clamoring for recognition, and the quickly coiling knot of need at her core. For an eternity of desire she fought that past. Hands locked now at the back of his neck, she closed her eyes, let her head fall back, and the world of sensual pleasure rendered her momentarily mindless. Her lips parted; her breathing was short. Ross continued his play, deriving his pleasure from hers.

But the tug-of-war blossomed into a skirmish as the craving of her body grew more demanding. It was a battle entirely within Chloe, driving her toward Ross even against her better judgment, that grew bolder by the minute. Sensing only the physical need that mirrored his own, Ross gently brought her body forward. With her arms still about his neck, she rested her forehead against his chin, subconsciously offering him an entrance he hadn't had before.

Small explosions of delight flared through her when the slightly roughened skin of his fingers moved against the smooth flesh at her neckline, then slid within to touch and surround her breasts, warm, full, and straining against first the fabric, then his hand. His thumb and forefinger met at a nipple, coaxing it to further heights, driving her to even greater distraction, edging her passion beyond reason. In that split instant she knew of only one road to satisfaction.

"Come upstairs with me, Chloe," Ross rasped in a voice thick with need. "Let me love you. It's been so long, princess."

Later she was to realize that Ross had done no differently eleven years ago than she had done. Just as she had formed an image of him in her mind and held to it through the years, so he had done with her. In his mind she was still the princess she had been then. But not in hers. Unknowingly, he had forged that bitter shard of reality that kept history from repeating itself.

"No!" she cried urgently, straining back against the hands that continued to hold her, then lowering her voice to a more rational level. "No! I can't do that!" Suddenly awash with self-disdain, she trembled as the extent of her near-folly hit her.

"Can't?" he challenged hoarsely.

"Won't," she amended in a whisper, slowly, very slowly regaining her composure. Eleven years ago she hadn't refused him. Her virginity had never had a chance against the force of his appeal. But things were different now. *She* was different.

"Why, Chloe?"

She heard his hurt and sensed that it had little to do with pride. "I wish I could explain. . . ." Her voice faltered.

"Why can't you?" he probed solemnly. "I've seen that pained look in your eyes. At those moments—at this moment—you look unhappy. Is it something about me? Something about what happened eleven years ago?"

For those eleven long years Chloe had hidden a world of inner feelings from everyone around her. Even his prodding couldn't dent the wall.

"Here." He spoke more gently, the cadence of his breathing now back to normal. "Why don't you sit down? I'll make us some coffee. You can talk then."

"I don't want to talk, Ross. Some things are best left dead and buried." Her impulsive choice of words brought with them a shudder.

"Sit!" he commanded, nudging her into the chair she

had left. She sat, welcoming the respite for her unsteady legs, as Ross proceeded to clear the table, rinse everything, and perk a small pot of coffee. Her eye followed his movements almost incidentally. Her thoughts were far away in the world of what-if's. What if Crystal had won that toss of the coin? What if Crystal had set out to seduce Ross and then been quite totally seduced herself? Would Chloe now feel the same overwhelming guilt?

"How do you take it?" Ross asked, placing a steaming mug before her.

Snapping out of her semitrance, she held a hand up in refusal. "Black is fine. Thank you."

After lacing his own with milk and sugar, he reseated himself across from her. To his surprise, it was Chloe who spoke first. Though surprise quickly melded with comprehension, he listened patiently.

"You've come a long way in the business world since I saw you last, Ross. How did you manage it?"

He smiled. "You mean, how did I manage the transformation from 'far out' to 'far in'?"

Shrugging her agreement, she chuckled at his charm. But he went on with quiet conviction.

"In truth, I never was all that 'far out.' I went my own way for a while. I avoided money and its accumulation. I grew a beard because there wasn't modern plumbing where I was in Africa and I didn't particularly want to have to shave at dawn by the riverside. I wore jeans because they were comfortable, loose shirts likewise. After years of rigid discipline in school and at home, I wanted my freedom."

" 'Rigid discipline'?" she echoed in curiosity, realizing again how truly little she knew of Ross. Her forehead puckered beneath the fine fall of her raven tresses, center parted and flowing to either side of her face.

Ross eyed her with something akin to amusement. "You know, Chloe, considering that you gave yourself to the man the first time you met him . . ."

"Ross!" she gasped. "That's not fair! That night there were . . . extreme circumstances."

"Precisely," he drawled, his grin now mischievous, hinted at their earlier activity. Chloe, however, refused to let him rib her further.

"You know, Ross"—she mimicked his accusation—"you didn't know any more about me—at least, not *from* me—that night." But rather than turning the tables, she found herself more deeply incriminated.

Ross was clearly enjoying himself. "Neither of us did much talking, did we?"

She could only shake her head. To this day she recalled the only form of communion they'd shared. It had consisted of soft moans and caresses, of a hunger fiercely sated. The attraction had been overpowering! "Ross, I want you to know . . ." It seemed necessary to set him straight. ". . . I don't do that . . . as a rule. I mean, I don't make a habit of—"

"—jumping into bed with every guy that comes along?" Her thought was finished in a decidedly masculine voice. "I know that, Chloe." He smiled gently. "I told you that we had something special. Do you honestly think that *I* bed every attractive woman I run into?"

"Of course not," she denied as gently. "I just wanted you to know not to expect something I can't give."

"*Won't* give," he corrected a second time.

"The end result is the same. You understand, don't you?"

"No, Chloe, I don't. I hear you. I'm listening." He was sober. "And I'll respect your wish. But don't ask my understanding. You haven't given me a good reason to understand yet. Most women with your looks would have reached the point, at age twenty-nine, where they could recognize something deeper."

Chloe felt stymied. "What do my looks have to do with anything?" she asked in frustration, sensing that only the truth would satisfy Ross, knowing that she could not, as yet, give him that. This present course was mere diversion.

The amber gaze that touched her soft curves gave sufficient answer even before he spoke. "You're beautiful, Chloe. You've never married?"

"No."

"You must date often."

"I do have friends."

"*Male* friends?"

"Some."

"Chloe!" He seemed to be suddenly exasperated. "This is like pulling teeth! What I'm trying to find out is whether you're either *going* with someone, *living* with someone, *engaged* to someone . . ." He quieted abruptly. "Have I listed all the possibilities?"

For a fleeting moment Chloe imagined herself confronted by a strangely frustrated suitor. The thought, an oddly pleasant one, was reflected in her smile. "No, Ross. I date here and there, but there's no one special. I live alone."

"Ahhhh." Slowly he expelled the breath he'd held, and she half suspected it to be for effect. "Thank you," he added in facetious afterthought, then paused, his mind transporting him back over the years to the locale of their first meeting. "Tell me, do you go home much?"

Chloe flinched. "No." She held her voice steady, then backtracked in escape. "But what about you? You never did tell me about that 'rigid discipline' you suffered through."

Once again he humored her. "My father was heart-and-soul Army. A career man. Our house was run like a barracks. It was almost a treat when I was sent to military school."

"How awful! I mean . . . it's no wonder you . . . freaked out."

Ross's laugh filled the kitchen. "*Freaked out?* That's one from the old days!"

Guilty as charged, Chloe joined his laughter. "I'm sorry. It just slipped out. I can't remember the last time I used that term." The faint flush on her cheeks didn't fade with his rejoinder.

"Perhaps on the night you met me?" He stared at her for a long moment, then gazed pensively at the table as he raised a hand to rub the muscles at the back of his neck. Chloe followed the movement, half wishing she could do it for him. But *dangerous* was a mild word for *that* type of thing! Once danger had been a challenge. Now she wanted no further part of it.

Ross's soft confession broke into her thoughts. "I may have been pretty antiestablishment, at that. There was a certain amount of rebellion in me against routine and schedules and even expectations. I suppose I *wasn't* much different from the average flower child . . . except that *I knew* I'd be returning to the fold before long. I saw it for what it was—a period in my life when I could freely stretch my legs."

The figure of speech brought a chuckle from Chloe. Her smoky gaze fell to the floor, where a pair of well-shod feet, ankles crossed, extended well beyond her side of the table. "Hmmm, an awesome task." She quirked a brow, then looked back up to bring the discussion full circle. "So how *did* you become a successful businessman? You obviously didn't go into partnership with your dad. But you've come a long way in eleven years. President of the Hansen Corporation." She shook her head in amazement.

"I, too, had a mentor," he explained simply. "I worked for him through business school, then after. The business did well. I gradually acquired stock. When Sherman died two years ago he left me enough shares to give me the majority holding."

"Was the Rye Beach Complex your idea?"

"Actually, no. It was the baby of one of the other vice-presidents. Sherman seemed to feel it had merit."

"And you *don't?*" Considering the force of his presentation before the crowd that evening, she was startled.

"I do . . . with reservations."

"Why did *you* come up tonight then, rather than the VP who feels more strongly about it?"

Ross shrugged, as though it were unimportant. "He is . . . no longer with the corporation." That he felt no regret at the fact was obvious; that he had fired the man might easily have been true. As he sat before her, Chloe sensed the latent power in the man. A free spirit, he had called himself. Now he ruled a large and prominent corporation. With an iron hand? Intuitively, she knew not. He would use more subtle, though equally powerful, methods to reach his goals.

"What do you intend to do about it?" she asked carefully.

"About what?"

"The complex. You mentioned some doubts. Tonight's meeting must have raised others. Will you change your proposal?"

"No." His declaration was firmer, softer.

"*No?* Ross, to build the complex as planned would be really dumb environmentally!"

"'Dumb'?" he mocked with a grin, enjoying her anger.

His ability to put her down with one echoed word galled her. Exasperated, she threw her hands into the air and let them fall with a thud to the table. "I gave all the reasons in that auditorium and I won't repeat them now. Do you always go about your building projects so bullheadedly?"

"And what do you know about my building projects?" There was still a trace of amusement in his expression.

"Nothing." It was the truth. "I had only heard of the Hansen Corporation before tonight, but I knew very little about it. But if it's like ninety percent of other such enterprises, it puts the dollar bill before every other consideration."

"Not always." His voice carried a quiet note of warning, which she promptly ignored.

"Then you acknowledge that profit is your raison d'être?" Readying for battle, she had pulled herself up straighter. To her chagrin, Ross laughed.

"Chloe, I would never be where I am today if I didn't have an eye out for profit!"

Feeling suddenly and inexplicably betrayed, she stood up rigidly. "That's really pathetic, you know!" Her beleaguered mind flashed images of that tall, handsomely bearded man in jeans, boots, and a simple peasant shirt. "I would have thought that, with what you stood for at one time, you might have avoided such a crassly capitalistic attitude! You *have* sold out!" She shook her head, barely noticing that Ross had pushed his chair out and was slowly rising from it. Nor did she notice that his fists were clenched. "It just goes to show how terribly wrong one person can be in the judging of another . . . or how naive!"

"You don't know what you're talking about, Chloe!" he seethed, his words rumbling through the air, reverberating through her. "You didn't know me *then*, and you certainly don't know me *now!* When I returned from Africa that last time with my grungy denims, my dashiki, and my full-bearded presence"—his eyes narrowed to amber slits of anger—"it took me all of a week to shuck them. And do you know why?" He paused, his gaze spearing her. "*Do you?*"

Only when she shook her head did he go on. "Because I saw that there was more narrow-mindedness, more prejudice, coming from the mouths of the hippie generation than anywhere else. Because of my appearance, I was assumed to be one of them—until they discovered that I didn't always think the way they did, that I had a mind of my own. The true sign of a liberal, Chloe, is accepting people for their very differences, respecting their *right* to *be* different. They—all those others who prided themselves on being nonconformists —declared all-out war on the establishment. And what happened?"

Without waiting for her response he bulldozed on, his voice low but relentless, his gaze no less intense. He leaned forward, putting his hands on the table.

"When was the last time you saw a flower child? Hmm? They've vanished. Disbanded. Lost the war." The pause he took was for a deep breath. "Well, I haven't lost. I'm working from *within* to change things. Did that ever occur to you, Chloe? You've been so quick to label me first one way, then the other. Did it ever occur to you that your picture wasn't even skin deep, that there's a *me* underneath it all?"

It was an eternity before Chloe felt capable of speech. She certainly *didn't* know Ross; this scathing speech he'd delivered represented a wholly new side of him. And he was right!

"I'm sorry, Ross." She spoke with quiet conviction. "It was wrong of me to do that. I'm not *always* that way." She tried a smile in apology. To her intense relief, it seemed to work. His features gradually softened.

"Only with me, eh?" He inhaled deeply and stood tall, holding his breath for a minute while his head fell back, then releasing it as his eyes met hers.

She felt suitably contrite and suddenly very drained. "You have this knack for bringing out the extreme in me. I guess I'm just tired. It's late." An exaggerated glance toward the bold face of Ross's watch told her exactly *how* late. "Oh, Lord! It's two in the morning!" With a gasp, she looked toward the ceiling. Her voice was a hoarse whisper. "Do you think we've woken anyone up?"

Ross's chiding was gentle. "No need to whisper now. If our yelling didn't wake 'em, nothing will." Absently, he took the two empty coffee cups and brought them to the sink.

With a cloth Chloe wiped off the table. "If it hadn't been for that battery"—she spoke her thoughts aloud, unthinkingly—"I'd have been back home in bed by now."

"Instead," his voice teased, "we've had a chance to get reacquain—ah, acquainted."

Chloe stopped what she was doing in midstroke, straightened, then balled the cloth in her hand. Acquainted was one thing; where would they go from there? The physical attraction that had been rekindled with a vengeance earlier weighed heavily on her.

"Uh-uh, now, Chloe." He was close behind her. "Just relax." Her gaze shot back over her shoulder to a white-shirted chest. How did he know? "I can feel it in the air—that whatever-it-is that disturbs you." He took the cloth from her and deftly tossed it into the sink. "I'm not going to pounce. I'll simply walk you to your room." He did, halting on the threshold. "The manager said he'd leave plenty of towels. I wish I could offer you something else. You seem to be without those . . . things"—to her astonishment, his neck took on a crimson tinge—". . . that most women can't do without."

She smiled at his vulnerability and at his concern. "I don't need anything."

"A shirt? Would you like a fresh shirt of mine . . . in place of a . . ."

"Negligee?" Her smile widened. "No, thanks, Ross. If the sheets are clean, they'll be covering enough." She purposely ignored his sharp intake of breath. "But, Ross? I've *got* to get an early start in the morning."

Forcing a fast recovery, he nodded. "I called the garage while you were preparing our dinner and left a message. They'll be at your car no later than eight. Is that *too* early?"

"Lord, no! I've got to call Lee, my partner, anyway. There's a small matter of an appointment at nine."

"Will she fill in for you?" he asked innocently.

Just as innocently, she answered, "No. He'll have work of his own to do." She stifled a grin at Ross's attempt to nonchalantly assimilate her correction. "He'll simply cancel and explain for me. I'll reschedule as soon as I get back."

Ross gnawed at his lower lip, nodding down at her from a height that filled the doorway. There was obviously more that he wanted to say but, much as Chloe was vaguely curious, she dared not invite his lingering presence. Dangerous. Very dangerous. Yet when, with a quiet "Good night," he turned and headed down the stairs to his own room, she felt distinctly disappointed. Though one small voice within recalled the tragic outcome of her last serious flirtation with danger, another voice wondered whether this particular risk might be worth it.

Not only had the night manager left extra towels, he'd also provided her with a Care package of other goodies tailor-made for the stranded motorist. There was a toothbrush, as well as toothpaste, a comb, soap, and, luxury of luxuries, an envelope of bubble-bath powder.

Chloe's lips curved up in a smile of mischief. She'd had her share of tension today; now she would release it. The devil could take the hour; *she* would take a long, hot bath! It had been ages since she'd done so. Why not! Several deft flicks of her wrist sent a full stream of hot water into the long porcelain tub, which stood, in keeping with the vintage aura of the inn itself, on four clawed feet. Feeling perfectly scandalous, she sprinkled the entire contents of the envelope beneath the steaming flow. It was only when the water had reached a naughty height that she finally turned it off.

Moments later she was immersed up to her neck in bubbles. With her hair draped over the lip of the tub, she closed her eyes and surrendered to pleasure. Was it true what they said about the subconscious urge to return to the womb? Was this what it had been like—warm and all-enveloping, floating lightly?

The womb, however, was not where she wished most to be at that moment. Rather, she thought of Ross's arms as he had held her earlier that night, of his lips as he'd kissed her, his strong body as it had supported her. A sense of euphoria stole through her, allowing her, for the first time since the initial shock of Ross's reappearance had hit, to think back on the full story of that night eleven years ago.

It had been the holiday recess. She and Crystal had returned from their first semester at the university to spend Thanksgiving with the family. The boys were gathered: Allan from Denver, Chris from Chicago, Tim from St. Louis—from their respective subdivisions of the MacDaniel domain. They had spent a typically revel-filled Thanksgiving Day, complete with gargantuan offerings of turkey, stuffing, salads and vegetables and fruit molds, pies and cakes and other goodies, not to mention the company of aunts and uncles and cousins galore. It had been later that night that she and Crystal had dropped in at Sandra's house, where a party had been in progress.

Sandra had been their best friend through their relatively carefree high school years. They hadn't seen her since September, since she'd left to go to college in New York, where her older brother lived.

Ross was a friend of that brother. From the moment Chloe set foot into the Brownings' living room that night her eye had been drawn to him. He had seemed to represent all the things she'd never known—nonconformity, independence, singularity. Even in a crowd, he stood out. Sandra had said he was in the Peace Corps, stationed in Africa. He was tall and breathtakingly attractive in a wholly new and exciting way for Chloe. Crystal had sensed it, too.

"Gorgeous, isn't he?" she had whispered for the ears of her twin alone.

"I'll say. What do you think he's doing here?"

"That's a dumb question," Crystal had scolded hoarsely. Neither of them could tear their eyes away from him. "He's visiting the Brownings, just like we are."

"Not bad! Do you think he's got a girl?"

"A guy like that? Make it girls. He's oozing virility—or hadn't you noticed?"

"I noticed! I noticed!" Chloe had drawled into her sister's ear. "Do you think he'll notice *us?*"

"Why not? We're rich and beautiful and sexy—"

"—and young."

Crystal had bristled. "What's *that* got to do with anything?"

"If he's Sammy's friend, Crystal, he's got to be at least ten years older than we are! You don't really think he'd be interested, do you?"

"God, Chloe! Are you a stick-in-the-mud! Of course he'll be interested. Men like freshness. And we *are* rich and beauti—"

"I know, I know, I heard you before." Chloe's chiding whisper had interrupted the litany. "It gets boring." The sudden disdain she'd felt at her sister's arrogance had surprised her. So often they had shared it. As the babies of the family—and twins, at that—they'd been reared like royalty. For the first time, however, Chloe wondered whether men like this stranger were attracted to royalty. Was being rich and beautiful and sexy all that mattered? Something had told her that this divine-looking man would seek more. Something in his gaze as he slowly turned it their way.

"Wow! I'm going after him," Crystal had announced under her breath.

"Oh, no. It's my turn," Chloe had countered, driven to match her sister's determination. "You got Roger. This one's mine."

"He won't want a stick-in-the-mud. *You* think we're too young for him."

"*I've* changed my mind. Besides, it's *me* he's looking at, not you."

"The choice is arbitrary," Crystal had argued defensively. "We look exactly alike."

"All of a sudden we look *exactly* alike?" Chloe had choked. "What about that 'added bit of spice' you usually claim to have? What about that 'glow of vulnerability' that, as the last born, you claim?"

Crystal's nose had crinkled. "Oh, he can't see all that at this distance."

But Chloe had been softly vehement. "I have a feeling about him."

"You *always* have feelings about people. *I'm* the doer. Remember?"

"Not this time."

"Chloe . . ."Crystal had warned in a singsong murmur.

"Crystal . . ." Chloe had echoed the tune. "We'll toss a coin." She decided for them both. "Heads, I win."

Crystal's eyes had narrowed. *"I'll* do the tossing. You *always* seem to win."

It was true. While Crystal, with her heightened impishness and propensity for instigating trouble, was often at the fore in their mischief-making, Chloe invariably won the toss of the coin. And with good reason. As the more levelheaded of the two, she was expected to be the one to produce the coin. It came from a secret fold in her wallet and served no other purpose than this. It would never have passed for currency—for it had two heads. But Crystal never knew that, not even when she did the tossing herself.

And so, with the keenest of amber eyes pulling her forward magnetically, Chloe had approached the mysterious man of the love generation. Initial silence had given way to the exchange of smiles, then names. There was brief small talk, belying the soul-stopping set of vibrations that sizzled through the air between them. The party had paled then. Friends forgotten, they had wandered onto the patio, then taken refuge by the pool, later moving on to the sloping lawn of Sandra's parents' estate.

Chloe shifted slowly in the tub, eyes closed, moving as in a trance. The heat of the water had dissipated, but was replaced by the heat of her body as she remembered. It had been warm that night. The crescent of the moon had been brilliant, echoed in the white smile that had split Ross's dark beard as he'd looked down at her.

"You're a vision, Chloe," he had whispered, sharing her fascination. "Are you real?"

"I'm real," she had whispered back, shy and then uncharacteristically tongue-tied.

But further words had been unnecessary. The guest house in which Ross was staying had been on a far corner of the estate. He'd taken her there, pausing along the way to kiss her, to assure her with a protective embrace that he would not hurt her. He'd been a masterful lover, so very gentle as he'd undressed her, so very subtle as he'd bared his man's body to her awed gaze, so very patient as he'd coaxed her to heights of desire, so very tender as he'd finally pierced the veil that had held the joys of womanhood from her. And joys they'd been. When tenderness and care had yielded to hard, fierce passion, she had soared with him, reveling in an ecstasy she'd never known before.

Ross's lovemaking had been a solemn, yet almost magical, experience. She would always cherish it as such.

Once again she stirred in the tub, suspended momentarily between the world of memories and the present. In a final indulgence, she moved her hand beneath the water, touching the skin Ross had touched, tracing the curves he had traced. Thoughts of him were fresh and near. Lips parted, she sighed her sensual delight.

It was at that moment that her back slipped against the

porcelain. With a jerk she sat quickly up, but not before the long strands of her hair had gotten wet.

Softly hissing her annoyance, she reached for a towel to wrap around her head, then soaped herself quickly and climbed out. What had been a lovely trip into the past had ended in abrupt frustration. And there was no promise of satisfaction for this clamoring knot of need within—just as there was no hope of respite from the guilt she still felt.

For the guilt was only in part related to the act of loving she'd known that night. Its other part was Crystal. Crystal—her twin. Crystal—her alter ego. Crystal—who had never known that same joy, but should have, should have at least once before her death such a short time later.

3

~~~~~~~~~~

The long raven ponytail bobbed gaily against her neck as Chloe jogged along the beach. Indian summer had come to Rhode Island, bringing with it bright sun and a heat that was unusual for a mid-October day. She wasn't about to complain, though. All too soon her daily run would require the added burden of a sweat suit, hat, and gloves. Now she delighted in the freedom of shorts and tank top, which allowed her slender arms and legs to breath as well of the sweet, moist ocean air. The sweat that dotted her brow trickled across her temple and down along her hairline by her ear. It glistened on her skin, adding an aesthetic glow.

As always when she ran, she thought. Two weeks. It had been two weeks since she had seen Ross Stephenson, since his stunning presence had popped into her life once more. He had a way of doing that, she mused, as she dodged a piece of driftwood that had been washed up and deposited by nature for an artistic soul to find.

The steady patter of her sneakers on the wet sand became even once again.

Eleven years ago he'd scored a thunderous coup, conquering her mind and body in a matter of a few mindless hours of loving. Though their encounter two weeks ago had been under vastly different circumstances, it had been, in its way, no less devastating.

The physical attraction between them hadn't diminished over the years. If anything, it was more awesome than before, if her recollection of that kiss in the kitchen of the Wayward Sailor was correct. *How could she have let herself go like that?* It was a question that had nagged at her incessantly, and she found herself growing ill-tempered all over again. It had been *his* fault, damn it! He *must* have known how he would affect her. He must have planned it *all*—right down to his sudden disappearance the next morning.

Her thoughts sped back to that morning. A maid had kindly awakened her at seven, tactfully ignoring her grogginess to put a pot of fresh coffee and a plate of sweet rolls on the small stand by her bed before scurrying back out. Chloe hadn't known quite what to expect— whether Ross would wake her himself or meet her downstairs for breakfast. She'd assumed, at the very least, that he would have been the one to drive her back to her car that morning.

It was therefore a surprise to find, on reaching the front desk in a fairly revived, though mildly testy, state, that Ross had already checked out. Instant disappointment gave rise to self-reproach. There was no cause for regret. It was better this way, she had told herself. The previous night's brief sojourn in his arms spoke all too clearly of her vulnerability. His passion was too beautiful a thing, sweeping her wildly into indescribable and utterly breathtaking realms of sensation. She didn't deserve such pleasure; it was enough to be alive. No, she didn't deserve Ross's—or any other man's—loving. Far better that he should be gone from her life for good!

When the day manager had handed her Ross's note, however, her momentary calm had been shattered. "Chloe," he had scrawled in a bold hand, "Had to leave to catch the early plane. Your car is taken care of. The Inn will take you there." It was signed, "Love, Ross." and was punctuated with a firm period, symbolic of a statement of fact. *Love.* Had that simply been a figure of speech? How could he have used the word so blithely?

But *that* had been the least of it! Already on edge, she had been instantly annoyed to find that Ross had paid, in full, her tab at the Inn *and* the cost of a new battery and its installation. Had he suspected, *wanted* her to feel indebted to him? Had he purposely planted those tiny bugs in her ear, those small guarantees that she'd have to remember him?

Her panting increased in proportion to the heat as she ran on, struggling to exorcise the demon of Ross Stephenson from her mind. It was not to be, however. His image, dark and compelling, had laid seige to her imagination and would not be banished.

Her pride had made her quick to react to his takeover of her welfare on that trip to Rye. She was, after all, independent and self-sufficient. Without delay, upon her return to Little Compton that morning, she had obtained the address of the Hansen Corporation. A check went out in the mail that day, with a note that had been much less personal than his, a note written in sheer self-defense.

"Enclosed is a check to cover the expenses I incurred last night and this morning. Chloe MacDaniel." Fortunately, Ross had been unable to see the tension in her lips as she sealed the note. Fortunately, he was unaware of the second thoughts she had had about the entire matter. Oh, there had been no question in her mind but that she would repay him. But if she had been honest with herself, she would have recognized the curiosity she'd felt, then squelched, at the discovery that Ross and his office were located in New York. She would have acknowledged that faint bit of disappointment that once again she had acted to sever her ties with him. She would have pondered the reason why his use of the word *love* bothered her so.

There seemed to her only one clear fact. The guilt she still felt over her sister's death and the circumstances surrounding it was all-encompassing. She had neither the capacity to love a man—Ross—as he should be loved, nor the right. If Crystal had lived life without that, so should she.

Yes, it was for the best that she never see Ross again. With firm resolve she made a gentle semicircle and jogged more slowly back toward where she had left her towel on the rocks to the sea side of her home.

As she approached, however, it wasn't the house that caught her eye but the tall figure that had moved away from it and begun to walk to the beach. "Oh, no!" she gasped, stopping short. "It can't be . . ."

But it was. He was dressed in casual slacks of navy blue and a plaid sports shirt unbuttoned at the neck and rolled up above the elbows. The thickness of his hair tumbled in dark disarray across his brow. Even from a distance he looked threatening in an almost divine kind of way. Chloe bristled as she walked on.

Despite her slowed pace, her pulse raced as if in the middle of a final sprint. He must have seen her from the first, perhaps had stood by the living room window until she'd come into sight. *Damn!* If only Lee hadn't been there to answer the door, he might have turned around and left. Now she was caught—and annoyed.

Her chin was cocked in defiance as she drew nearer. Ross had stopped and made no move to meet her halfway, but followed her with his relentless gaze. His stance held both a bit of anger and a touch of the imperious. Despite his dress, he looked oddly formal. Accordingly, she came to a halt before him, nodded, and offered a polite "Ross" in greeting, before shifting beyond him to retrieve her towel. She was unprepared for his outburst.

"What in the hell did you do it for, Chloe?" His voice held just the chill she needed after her exertion.

"Do what?" She straightened slowly, the towel forgotten.

His amber intensity bore into her. "Send that check. You didn't lose a minute, did you? You must have had it in the mail that same afternoon."

"And why not?" She frowned, perplexed by his reaction.

"There was no need."

"*I* thought there was. *You* had no cause to pick up the check, either for the Inn or the new battery." Her indignation exploded in a low voice. "I *am* capable of taking care of myself, you know."

The muscle that worked in his jaw suggested displeasure. "Then it was a matter of principle?"

"I really hadn't meant it that way, Ross," she defended herself staunchly. "I simply saw it as *my* responsibility. It was kind of you to offer to pay, but I feel more comfortable this way. I wanted to take care of it myself."

"Is that how you intend to live the rest of your life—by yourself?" the deep voice challenged.

Chloe was stunned at the sudden turn of the conversation. "This is absurd!" she burst out, slamming her hands onto her hips. "You show up here, out of the blue, without so much as a civil hello, and put me on trial! I don't have to defend my life-style to you or anyone else!" She caught her breath and began to turn, then softened in confusion. "Why *are* you here, Ross? Did you come all the way from Park Avenue to call me out for repaying your . . . loan? Little Compton is on the way to nowhere! We're at the tip of a peninsula. So don't tell me that you were just passing through."

"No," he began, his features remaining relaxed despite the acuity of his gaze. "I wanted to see you."

Chloe felt suddenly uncomfortable. With as much nonchalance as she could muster, she bent for her towel, then straightened with it in hand. "You could have called . . . if you wanted to discuss the Rye Beach Complex. Nothing has happened since the meeting. Nothing much will happen until the referendum in November. Unless, of course, you alter your proposal." Satisfied with her minor dig, she began to mop at the dampness of her face and neck, mindless of the fact that it was tension that now caused her clamminess.

Ross ignored her barb. "I'm not here on business, Chloe." His gaze didn't waver. "It's you I want to see."

"That's a mistake," she whispered, hearing the pain in her voice as it cut through her insides.

His retort was cushioned in similar softness. "Then once more we differ in opinion. Look"—he sighed— "can we walk? Your house seemed pretty crowded. I'd like to talk."

All too aware of the tingling of her nerve ends, she shook her head, then tore her gaze from his and looked out to sea. "It's not a good idea, Ross." She clung stubbornly to a resolve that had already, to her dismay, begun to erode. "If it has something to do with the complex, I'd be glad to talk. Anything else . . ."

"What are you afraid of, Chloe?" he said, confronting her. "I see the same fear in you now that I saw two weeks ago. What is it?"

"Nothing," she lied quickly, only to be caught by the chin and forced to look back up at his handsome features.

"Then what can be the harm in talking? What can be so awful about walking along the beach with me for a few minutes? After all, you've got a whole crew in there"

—his dark head nodded back toward the house—"to come if you scream."

"I won't scream," she spoke accordingly softly as she blushed lightly. "It's not my style."

For long moments he analyzed her statement and its accompanying poise. "Maybe that's your problem," he finally decided. "You're too composed. Maybe you need a good yell and scream to let it all out."

"Let *what* all out?" *God*, she wondered in a panic, *was she that transparent? Could he see everything* whirling around in her mind?

"Come on." He took her arm. "Let's take a walk." Gently he pulled her into step beside him. Despite misgivings that grew with each passing moment, she yielded. After all, what harm *could* come from a walk on the beach? One surreptitious glance up through her dark fringe of lashes provided the answer instantly. The magnetism was there in all its force, emanating from Ross, tugging at her. If only they had never met before, there might have been hope.

"What if," he echoed her thoughts with uncanny precision, "we had never met before? Would you feel differently?"

It was a difficult question, one she had struggled with long before now.

"Perhaps." Her hands clutched tightly at the ends of the towel that circled her neck. "Would you?" some inner voice made her ask, even against her will.

"No." There was no hesitancy in his response. "I saw a woman two weeks ago who interested me. I would be here regardless. It's just . . ."

As Chloe waited for his voice to pick up again, their paths crisscrossed her earlier footprints. Ross easily measured his pace to hers. "It's just . . . what?" she prodded at last.

The lithe body beside her halted; she went a step further, then turned to face him. He seemed to deliberate intently. "It's just"—his dark brows drew together —"that, having shared what we did eleven years ago, I feel that much more . . . justified . . ."

Something in his tone sent tremors of dismay through her. Though still soft, her voice began to rise in pitch, as it often did when she was distressed. "Are you saying that you feel *guilty,* so long after the fact? Is that why you've come? To ease some long-harbored guilt? Where were you *then?*" she burst out impulsively. "Where were you when I—"

With a gasp she cut herself off. For the very first time she wondered what *might* have happened had Ross been with her at the time of Crystal's death. It had been late Saturday night, a mere two days after Thanksgiving, when she and Crystal had argued, Crystal had raced off in her car, the accident had happened. By that time Ross had been well on his way back to Africa. What if he had been with her through the ordeal? Would things have been different? But he *hadn't* been with her; there was no changing that fact. Why, then, had she suddenly blurted out the thought? Why? Why now? *Why in front of Ross?*

Though Ross couldn't have missed her torment, his face registered confusion. It was temporarily put aside, however, when she put her hand to her forehead and closed her eyes for a moment in search of composure.

"Over there," he said quickly. "Those rocks. You should sit down."

"I'm all right—" she protested, only to be soundly interrupted.

"Then *I* want to sit down! Indulge me!" he barked impatiently, leading her to a jagged outcropping of rocks low enough at its base for them to find comfortable perches.

"All right, now." He quietly broached the topic foremost in his mind. "Why don't you tell me about that night—and *stop* looking at me as though I'm crazy! You know exactly what I'm talking about. I know what *I* experienced that night. I'd like to hear what *you* did."

"Oh, Ross," she sighed wearily. "I don't really want to go into this." Her eye caught the graceful takeoff of a tern from the salt-soaked beach and she turned to the glory of the weather. "It's too beautiful to rehash the past."

"The past had its moments of beauty, too," he coaxed her in calm but pointed argument.

Her head snapped back, but the warmth of his gaze cut off the sharp retort that might have come. Suddenly it seemed pointless to resist his request. It was merely a matter of choosing the proper words. With an unconsciously plaintive haze shadowing her features, she acquiesced. "I suppose you're right."

"You *suppose?*"

"You *are* right," she amended softly. "The past did have its moments. And, yes, they were beautiful." There was a dreamy quality in her voice now as she traversed the years back to *that night.*

"Chloe, tell me." He seized on her apparent willingness, though he kept his hands firmly grasping the stone on either side of him. "Had you intended it to happen? When you first came toward me from the far side of that room, had you *hoped* that we'd end up in bed?"

"Beforehand?" She looked up in shock, then cringed. "No!" Her voice lowered with her eyes. "I had never done anything like that before. Oh, we had dated plenty and went to our share of parties. But we had never . . . that is," she stammered, "neither of us had . . . ah, I mean, *I* had never . . ."

"I know." He rescued her from her floundering, daring to touch her cheek with the back of his fingers. Chloe's face tilted instinctively toward his touch until she caught herself and stiffened. It was only at moments of weakness that she lapsed into the old, familiar "we" and "our" of her childhood.

"Were you sorry you did it?" His voice was low, urgent.

"No! . . . Yes! . . . Oh, I don't know," she finally ended in a whisper, tugging at the towel draped about her neck with clenched hands. "I can't give you a simple yes or no. The act itself"—she cleared her throat awkwardly—"I have never regretted. It *was* beautiful." Her gray eyes were luminous when they met his steady gaze.

"Then what is it about me that makes you so uncomfortable?"

The ensuing silence was rich with the sounds of the shore—the lapping of the waves, the cry of the gulls, the rustle of the breeze in the drying leaves of the wild honeysuckle. Each was a soothing balm, yet Chloe was still tense.

"Your presence brings back memories of a holiday weekend that was, in the end, tragic for me." She finally breathed the truth.

"Your sister's death."

Her gaze shot to his. *"You knew?"* He knew, yet he hadn't tried to contact her?

The dark sheen of his hair captured the golden rays of the slow-setting sun. "Yes, I knew—but not until well after I'd returned to Africa." Then, as though reading her hurt, he went on. "I didn't feel then that it was my place to contact you."

"Why not?" she exploded spontaneously. Considering his present persistence, that earlier detachment puzzled her.

"In the first place," he began, "it was pitifully long after the fact that I learned of it. Sammy wrote me the news in a letter the following spring." He seemed to hesitate, wrestling with his own demons. "It was only then that I had dared ask him about you."

"But why?" she cried impetuously, and he gave in to his anger.

"You weren't the only one to have afterthoughts of that night, Chloe! From what I could see I had wickedly seduced the virgin daughter of my host's best friend. I was twenty-seven. You were eighteen. I should have known better. But the worst of it was that I was glad I *hadn't* known better." He spoke more softly. "The memory of that night helped me through many a lonely night afterward!"

"Oh, Ross," Chloe whispered, unaware of the poignant look of longing in her eyes, "I wish it hadn't." Slowly, she shook her head. "It's too late to go back."

"I don't want to go back," he returned quickly. "I want to go ahead. That's why I'm here."

Anguished, she looked down. "It's no good. I can't."

"Can't—or won't?" His anger startled her. "We've been through this before, Chloe. Well"—he caught his breath as his tone grew gentler, though no less insistent —"believe this. I may have been immature eleven years ago, running away from something that frightened me, but I won't make the same mistake twice. It was fate that brought us together up at Rye Beach, and I'll be damned if I'm going to let you get away. I've made it my business to find out every possible thing I could about you during the past two weeks. And I know what happened to Crystal."

His words hung in the air like the sword of Damocles. The wide, bright pools of her eyes begged him to say no more. She bolstered the plea with her low whisper. "Then you can understand why I can't bear to think back on that time."

"It was an *accident*, Chloe! It wasn't your fault!"

"But *she* was the one who died."

"And you lived—is that it?" His deep accusation cut her to the quick. "You can't forgive yourself for that?"

Chloe felt every cell in her body rebel, gathering into an explosive feeling that demanded escape. "How can you be so cruel?" she gasped, jumping to her feet. Heart pounding its thunderous beat through every far inch of her being, she stared at him for a moment of agonized suspense before forcing her feet to move. Her faltering steps were slow at first, then gained speed as the force of habit took over, releasing her mind to its own world of torture as she jogged toward safer ground. But escape was not to be simple.

With an ease unhampered by his restrictive clothing, Ross caught up. His fingers curved around her elbow, bringing her own momentum into play against her. When she faced him at a full stop, he held her with a hand on either arm.

"I'm trying to be honest, Chloe."

"But it *hurts*, Ross. Can't you see that? *It hurts!*"

The hurt was etched in her every feature; he couldn't have missed it. It brimmed in the slate gray of her eyes, molded the pale hollows of her cheeks, found an outlet in the teeth digging into the fullness of her lower lip.

"The only way the hurt will stop," he chided more gently, " is for you to put the past *behind* you and look toward the future."

His dark features blurred as her eyes filled with tears. It took every bit of her strength to contain them. "Do you think I haven't tried?" she blurted out brokenly. "Do you really think I've spent the past eleven years purposely living with a ghost—"

"Yes!" His amber eyes were suddenly aflame with vehemence. "You haven't resolved a *thing* in the eleven years, if that hurt in your eyes is for real. It's your punishment, isn't it? Your punishment for living."

"No," she whispered, shaking her head. "That's not true!"

"Not true?" he echoed in a voice strangely mellow. "Answer me one thing, Chloe. Have you been with another man since we were together?"

"That's none of your bus—"

"It *is* my business!" His hands had left her arms to

imprison her face, correctly anticipating her attempt to look away. Though he held her firm, his touch was gentle—too gentle to fight. "I was the first. It's *my* brand that shaped you. How many others were there?"

"That's vulgar!" In self-defense she lashed out. "Are you jealous as well as guilt-ridden? Well, I don't need either of those traits in the man in my life. I'm doing just fine without—without—" This time it was the depth of her own sorrow, awakened by Ross's nearness, that cut her off. Her limbs trembled, threatening to give way.

Sensing her need for support, Ross drew her slowly against him, pressing her cheek against his chest, wrapping his arms about her back. "Without love?" he asked, so softly that she might not have heard him had the word not been on the tip of her own tongue.

Incapable of speech for the moment, she simply breathed in the scent that was all male, all Ross. His heart beat steadily by her ear, gradually coaxing her own to slow. His arms enveloped her in comfort, lending her the strength she needed to overcome the passing weakness.

"I tried, Ross." She spoke softly, unsteadily at first. "I dated . . . I still do." It was easier not having to look at him, to suffer either his disapproval or any latent desire his gaze might hold. "I even tried to . . . to . . . go to bed . . . with one of them." She sighed, recalling the moment. "He concluded that I was . . . frigid."

A deep laugh erupted from Ross's throat, a laugh strangely hoarse. "That's ridiculous!" he crooned into the silken warmth of the dark hair pulled back from Chloe's face. But when he tipped her face up he felt her stiffen, almost in proof of the accusation. "Oh, no, you don't," he commanded softly, an instant before his mouth found hers. But she fought him then. Struggling to free herself from the band of his arms, she pushed against his chest with her hands, all the while trying to evade his lips.

He was not to be easily thwarted, however. The more

she squirmed, the more he steadied her. His lips moved over hers, commanding the response that would hint at the height of passion of which *he* knew her to be capable.

When her physical strength waned before his persistence, Chloe tried passivity. The last thing she wanted was a repeat of the night in New Hampshire or, worse, that fateful night back in New Orleans. She had no right, she told herself, no right!

"Come on, Chloe," Ross growled against her lips. "Ease up."

"Don't . . ."

Her mistake was in saying anything, for the meager parting of her lips gave him the opening he needed. From that point on she didn't have a chance. His lips and tongue invaded her mouth, spreading their moist sweetness into her. She told herself that it was simply a physical onslaught, yet even as her mind resisted, her body betrayed her, and she swayed toward him with a weakness totally different from that trembling moments earlier.

From some odd mechanism of defense, her mind went blank. It was as though the battle between long-nurtured guilt and long-denied desire had wrought a mental void. In that void there was nothing but Ross and his body, the lips that caressed her so masterfully, the arms that held her so gently, the legs that supported her with such manly strength.

Her response came slowly, materializing from that void that Ross had conquered. When her lips moved against his, it was in tasting, in sampling. The corners of his mouth, his firm lips, his tongue—one small nibble led to another until her kiss returned his with matching passion.

"Oh, Ross," she breathed raggedly when his lips left hers to trail fire along the sensitive cord of her neck. "Ross . . ." She had no idea why she called his name; she only knew that her lips would form no other word.

"That's it, princess."

"No . . ." *That word. That past.*

"Yes!" His breath warmed her ear. "You'll always be my princess, Chloe," he rasped softly, nibbling at her lobe between phrases. "It's got nothing to do with the past. Right now you *are* my princess." With a groan, he pressed her to him fiercely. She felt his desire as she tried to deny her own. But that same coil of need had formed to gnaw impatiently within her. What could she do? How could she fight him? Worse, how could she live with herself tomorrow? In an instant of mind-shattering upheaval she felt on the verge of losing control.

"*No!*" Her scream rent the air, shuddering back through her with such force that only Ross's arms kept her standing, and that only for a moment. As her body sagged against him, he eased himself down onto the sand, turning her to sit with her back against his chest, her knees bent and bounded by his. He said nothing, merely held her, his arms wrapped about her middle.

For her part, Chloe could not have moved. Drained by the emotional strain of the encounter, she closed her eyes and breathed in deeply of the slow-cooling air. It was an eon of silent companionship later when Ross finally spoke. To her surprise, his tone was humorous.

"Not bad . . . for a novice," he quipped in a voice deep and resonant.

"What?" She was totally off-balance.

"That scream. For someone who claims not to be prone to that type of release, you sure let loose!"

She *had* screamed! Chloe of the cool, calm exterior had actually screamed! A helpless grin crossed her face. "So I did," she murmured softly. "You have this way of doing the weirdest things to me." Weirdest of all, she mused, was the sense of peace that had momentarily settled over her.

"I certainly hope so!" came the drawled retort.

"Ross—"

"Uh-uh, Chloe. I've heard enough from you for a while. Now you listen to me."

"But—"

"Quiet!" he ordered her with mock sternness. "When I want your comment, I'll ask for it."

"You—umph!" The breath was forced from her by a sharp squeeze to her middle. She didn't try to speak again.

"That's better," he crooned against her ear. "Now, listen. I realize that you need time . . . and I'm prepared to give you that. But I'm not leaving. Not this time. I intend to get to know you, and I want you to get to know me." He paused, then spoke as though to himself. "We really blew it on that score last time." He recovered quickly, rubbing his chin against her temple in reminder of her presence in his arms now. "Yesterday was one thing, Chloe. This is today. And it's something very, very different."

For what seemed an eternity, they sat against one another in silence, looking out over the last of the sunset's flaming rays. At this moment Ross provided the only heat she needed. She was intensely aware of him—of his long legs, his strong arms, his broad chest, his warm breath. Much as she knew she had no right, she savored the peace of the moment.

Perhaps there *was* something different about today. Certainly they were eleven years older, maybe even worlds wiser. But yesterday could not be forgotten.

Crystal had been an intrinsic part of her life. To forget her would be wrong. It was more a matter of acceptance. Could she accept the past and learn to live with it?

"Well?" Ross's rich baritone hummed by her ear.

"Well, what?" She had reached her saturation point and simply couldn't continue to agonize. Ross was obviously as determined to pursue his cause as she was to evade it.

"Don't you have *anything* to say for yourself?" He nudged her ribs.

Her long pause was nearly as effective as the soul-deep breath she took. "So . . . now I'm allowed to speak?"

"Speak!" he growled playfully.

"That's such a beautiful sunset," she mused aloud. "It's a treat at this time of year, all warm and golden. Do you have any idea what would happen if the ozone layer were to be destroyed by the haphazard release of freon gas?"

4

~~~~~~~~~~

"Chlo . . . eee."

Ross had time neither to pursue the environmental quandary she had proposed nor to analyze Chloe's plunge into the scientific before the call of concern came from far down the beach.

"It's Lee," Chloe explained as she quickly recognized the figure of her partner loping toward where she and Ross sat. Ross made no move to hold her back when she slid from his grip and jumped to her feet.

The timing couldn't have been better. With those legs framing hers and the strength of that body begging for her appreciation, her diversion would have been temporary, at best. Lee's appearance was a godsend.

Vaguely aware that Ross, too, had risen, Chloe kept her eyes glued to the approaching figure. "You met Lee at the house, didn't you?"

Ross's voice was strangely gruff. "No. Some other . . . character . . . let me in and directed me to you. It must be some kind of a commune you live in."

His facetious analysis fell prey to Lee's booming call. "Is everything all right, Chloe?" He covered the last of the distance at a more cautious walk, making no effort to disguise his wariness of the equally wary-eyed man beside her. "It's getting dark. I had begun to worry."

Chloe absently clutched her left wrist, a habit dating back to the days when she wore a watch. Her tapered fingers easily circled the slim bone. "Oh, Lee," she gasped, "I'm sorry! I lost track of the time. We were going to—" Suddenly aware of the silent but alert interchange between the men, she interrupted her thought to ease the tension. "Lee, this is Ross Stephenson. We knew each other a long time ago. Ross heads the corporation responsible for the Rye Beach proposal." For the first time since Lee's arrival she turned to Ross, who continued to study Lee closely. "Ross, this is Lee Haight. Lee and I co-own ESE."

For a brief instant she had the strangest image of the two men squaring off against one another. Her quickening pulse echoed that fear, steadying only after Ross extended his hand and it was met by Lee's equally large one.

As she stood back in momentary observation, Chloe was astonished at the physical similarities between these two, each of whom had been in his way instrumental in the shaping of her life. Both were tall and lean; both were of an athletic build. Whereas Ross's dark hair had those faint wisps of gray at the sideburns, Lee's highlights were of a more auburn tone. Both men were tanned; both were inordinately good-looking. Only their dress distinguished their particular approaches to life. Whereas Ross was the image of the casual male of the more traditional school, Lee was, in appearance, reminiscent of that earlier, more nonconformist phase through which the other had passed. While Ross wore navy twill slacks, Lee sported hip-hugging blue denims. While Ross wore a natty sports shirt, Lee wore a T-shirt emblazoned with an apt "Earthman." Ross wore well-kept loafers and Lee had a pair of battered running shoes. And then there was that neatly trimmed beard of Lee's that stretched from ear to ear, much as Ross's had on the night Chloe had first set eyes on him. It had never occurred to her to compare the two men before, but on all counts the likeness was astounding.

As though once again reading her mind, Ross grinned slowly, an almost sly smile breaking through his earlier caution. "It looks like Chloe's taste in men hasn't changed all that much, after all," he drawled, with such lack of malice that Lee couldn't help but return the greeting in a similarly more relaxed vein.

"I intend to take that statement at its most positive, friend. This little lady is very near and dear to me." He threw a protective arm about Chloe's shoulder, drawing her to him in the usual possessive way of his that always pleased her—and did so even more now.

Lee's presence took the edge off the intense vulnerability she'd felt alone with Ross. She barely stifled a chuckle when Lee's challenge came forth. "Are you friend or foe?"

"Friend, by all means," was Ross's too emphatic reply.

"Then I take it you're not here on business," the other concluded aloud. "And you can't be 'passing through.'" This time Chloe's bright laugh could not be contained.

"I've been through all that with him, Lee." Her eyebrow arched gracefully. "He knows precisely where he is."

"Hmmm." Lee glanced her way. "Sounds ominous," he growled with mock sternness. When he looked once more at Ross, he was more serious. "How long are you in for?"

"I'd planned to spend the weekend here," Ross answered with a calm diametrically opposed to the sudden play of butterflies in Chloe's stomach. When his amber eyes beamed on her, the butterflies fluttered en masse. "That is, if Chloe is free."

Whether Lee sensed the commotion unleashed within Chloe by Ross's declaration, she would never know. She was, however, eternally grateful for the arm that tightened about her shoulders, narrowing Ross's gaze commensurately.

"You'll have a fight on your hands, Ross. I'm afraid to say that I've got a prior claim on her. Your corporation may be able to do without you for the weekend, but our much smaller one isn't quite so generous." Looking down at her, he made his point. "There were several calls for you."

"Oh?" she asked, frowning. When she'd left the house to jog, what seemed like hours ago, she'd assumed things would remain quiet.

Lee briefed her quietly. "Alabama called again on that toxic waste burning problem. I told them you'd have an answer for them by Monday."

Chloe nodded, sighing her uncertainty on the matter, then prodding further. "And the other calls?"

"Derry Township called on the lecture series at the community college—they want to know when the printed material will be ready to be copied. Jay called in from Pittsburgh to say that he should be back on Sunday, and Debbie will have the statistics on the sinkhole study for you to see tomorrow."

"Great!" she exclaimed. "She sure got that together quickly!" Turning to Ross, she explained. "Debbie is the newest member of the firm. She's just completed her degree work. Her working knowledge of computers is far superior to Lee's or mine." She paused, momentarily lost in her thoughts. "I'd still like to take more courses."

"Why don't you?" Ross broke in quietly.

"I don't have the time. Lee and I have really had to work hard during the past few years to make ESE a functioning enterprise. I think"—she cast a sidelong glance toward her partner—"we may finally be seeing the light at the end of the tunnel."

The grimace that met her gaze took her by surprise. Where she had expected agreement, she found sudden doubt. *"That's* another point of discussion for the weekend," Lee informed her softly, squeezing her arm for a final time before releasing her. "But, look, it's getting dark. Why don't we carry on inside. Will you stay for dinner, Ross?"

Chloe bent to retie a shoelace that needed no retying. *Can it, Lee. The last thing the man needs is encouragement!* In her mind the only sure route to survival still seemed to rest in Ross's return to the ranks of history. He, however, had other ideas.

"That would be fine." He accepted Lee's invitation with calm gratitude. Only Chloe sensed something amiss. Standing to join the others in the walk back down the beach to her house, she found Ross's expression filled with bridled tension. Their gazes met and locked, clashing in silent battle. Once again she was grateful for Lee's presence—until he excused himself abruptly.

"I've got some great wine in the cellar, Chloe." He grinned. "The steaks are already on the counter. Why don't you take another one from the freezer? I'll meet you in the kitchen." And with that he left them.

Before she could regroup after Lee's escape Ross had pulled her to a halt. This time his hand was wrapped around her swathe of silky black ponytail.

"And what was *that* all about, Chloe?" he growled deeply, the line of his chin tightening in consternation. "I thought you lived alone? At least, that was the story you gave me."

"It's true." Staring straight ahead, she held herself rigidly.

Ross moved closer, his face hovering intimately above hers. "Then why is that fellow so damned *at home* in your house? He sounds as though he's the live-in chef—between the wine and the steaks. What other services does he perform?"

Incensed both by his implication and his lack of trust, Chloe balled her fists. "He's good enough to bring the trash to the dump once a week and put on the storm windows when winter comes and pump out the basement when it floods. In addition to which," she ground out through clenched teeth, *"his office* is located here, as is *mine,* and the *rest* of ESE." Risking pain in her scalp, she angled her head toward him. "I thought you learned something about me this week. It's a simple fact that the address of the headquarters of ESE and my own home address are the same." To her relief, the pain never materialized. Ross had released her hair at some unknown point during her tirade.

Both his expression and his voice softened. "I know that. I didn't bother to look up the home address of your partner, though. For all I knew he lived here with you."

"But I told you I lived alone!" With an impatience unusual to her, Chloe stalked onward toward the house in question. Ross materialized beside her in an instant.

"Where *does* he live?"

"Over there." Her slim forefinger pointed to a smaller house, further back from the beach, but no more than several hundred yards from Chloe's.

"How convenient," he mused dryly.

When she halted in her tracks this time, it was at her own command. Again Ross had driven her to new heights of temper. "It happens to be *very* convenient!" Slamming her hands onto her hips, she glared at the all-too-handsome face, which, to her chagrin, seemed suddenly amused. "He's a good friend, an able geologist, and a very trusting soul." The last she drawled in implicit accusation. When Ross dared to smile, she exploded. "And what is so funny?"

"Not funny." He laughed nonetheless. "Refreshing.

The way you seem to have repressed so many things over the years, I'm actually relieved that you can be so outspoken. But then, you were quite good up there at Rye Beach."

"Quite good?" she exclaimed. "I'll have you know that you'd better start rethinking those plans or the citizens of the county are going to vote down your entire project. And it didn't have as much to do with my being 'good' as with the simple truth of my arguments."

"Shhhh. Calm down," he cooed, continuing the walk toward the house, bringing her along with a feather touch of his hand at the back of her waist. "That was one of the things I had wanted to discuss this weekend."

"You did?" She eyed him skeptically. "I thought this was a strictly personal visit."

"It is. This is a personal business matter."

With a deep breath, she rolled her eyes skyward. "A personal business matter? Lord help me! What next?" The faint pressure of his hand on her back was ample suggestion. "Forget I asked that. A personal business matter. All right, we can discuss it during dinner."

"I was hoping," he stated with renewed confidence, "to discuss it in a more private meeting. Actually, I'd had every intention of taking you *out* to dinner. Alone."

"You should have called first."

"And would you have accepted if I had called?"

"No," she admitted softly, her anger spent. "Lee and I have a standing dinner meeting every Friday night to review the week's happenings."

They had reached the foot of the fieldstone steps that led to Chloe's back porch. Ross paused on the first step. "And those others I saw here this afternoon. Who were they?"

"They're workers on our various projects."

"Partners in the firm?"

She shook her head. "We hire a number of part-time people—mostly students, particularly master's candidates from schools like the University of Rhode Island and Brown University."

The pale blue of dusk was quickly giving way to the darker purples of evening in the star-filled sky. Ross's features were lit only by the golden light spilling through the kitchen window. Its lines more clearly cut, his profile was more distinct now than the fuller light of day had allowed. She found herself carefully studying this new side of him, drawn irresistibly to its dramatic appeal. When he smiled, the crow's-feet at the corners of his eyes crinkled in an endearing way.

"I admire you for your dedication . . . and that of the people you work with."

She studied him for a moment longer. "Is that wistfulness I hear?"

His chuckle was poignant in its way. "Perhaps. There are times . . . ach, well . . . that's another matter."

When she would have prodded, Lee's shout jarred her. "Chloe!" Her head shot toward the kitchen door. "Where are the matches? The pilot light is out on the broiler. I can't get it lit!"

"And here I thought *he* was the one who always came to *your* rescue, princess." Ross leaned close to murmur softly in her ear. When she turned to defend Lee, it was Ross's lips that were a breath from hers, his eyes that reflected their glow onto her, his body that warmed her now that the heat of the day had dissipated.

Mouth suddenly dry, she swallowed convulsively. "I—I think I'd better give him a hand. Pray we're not out of matches!" Her whisper was an attempt at humor. Ross had no way of knowing the truth underlying her quip. Indeed, Lee was a willing handyman—able, in nine cases out of ten. It was the tenth over which the two partners had a running gag. Chloe was convinced—and had informed Lee as much—that his occasional flub was intentional, a near-blatant reminder that *he* needed *her*. To this day he hadn't denied the claim. And considering all else the man offered Chloe, the least she could do was to come to *his* aid when he felt the need, as now. Without further hesitation she ran up the steps. It was only when she had reached the top and started for the door that Ross caught her hand and deftly passed her something. Surprised, she looked down at the book of matches.

"You smoke?" she asked on impulse.

"Actually," he responded with a wry twist of his lips, "I carry matches around with me just for that occasional pilot light that goes out."

"*Do* you smoke?"

"Through my ears . . . when I'm angry."

"*Do you?*"

"Smoke? No."

"That's good!" she exclaimed with a bold sigh of relief.

"Oh?" An eyebrow quirked with his question.

"This is strictly a nonsmoking house. If you wanted to smoke you'd have to sneak one in the john . . . or stay out here with the chipmunks."

"That's quite a choice. I guess I'm lucky I *don't* smoke. As it is," he teased her wickedly, "my only vice is sex. Do we have to sneak that in the john, too?"

It took every bit of her self-discipline to camouflage her helpless grin with a sterner facade. "Impossible . . ." she muttered softly, pulling the screen open and taking refuge in the kitchen, where her human buffer awaited her doting assistance.

Ironically, Lee's crisis was resolved just as Chloe's alarm sounded. For several moments there on the back porch, she realized with growing concern, she had forgotten who Ross was, what he was to her. He had been a handsome man, charming, with a sense of humor and a quick response to her own. *Thank heavens for Lee!*

It was a prayer of thanksgiving she offered more than once during the evening that followed. Lee was a perfect host, taking responsibility for the conversation during those periods when Chloe tuned out to privately contemplate Ross. She trembled to think what would have happened had she and Ross been alone in the house this night. Vulnerability . . . susceptibility. Whatever it was, Ross was a threat.

It had begun when she'd left the two men to deal with each other and dinner while she showered and changed into a pair of comfortable jeans and a western-style blouse replete with breast pockets, rolled sleeves, and a decoratively stitched yoke, both front and back. Her intent had been to be cool and at ease. The finished product, however, was one of homespun femininity. Had it been the pale pink hue of the blouse, she was later to ask herself? Or the way the seasoned denims outlined her slender hips? Whatever it was, it caught Ross's attention. Her first step into the living room, where the men were nursing drinks as the steaks grilled, brought Ross's eyes toward her for a thorough perusal, top to toe, that set her pulse hammering. It was downhill from there, at least where Chloe's peace of mind was concerned.

The talk centered on business matters. Sitting quietly ensconced in her peacock chair, Chloe learned that Ross's headquarters were indeed in New York, but that corporate branches had been opened in the South and West as well.

"You must live out of a suitcase a good deal of your time," she had emerged from her pensiveness to observe.

"I'm used to that. Don't forget, when I was a kid my family was shuttled here and there by the Army." At Lee's prodding, Ross had elaborated on his background, but Chloe's mind wandered. He had *never* settled down? Would he *ever*? How could a man as compelling and attractive as he was have avoided the lure of a wife, a home, a family? Her gaze swept his features in raw admiration, to be caught in the act when Ross smiled knowingly.

It was like that for much of the evening. Lee talked with

Ross, Ross with Lee, and Chloe joined them when she felt able. For the most part, however, she tried quietly to stem the rising attraction she felt for Ross. Why Ross? she asked herself at one point, when the two men had left to explore the offices adjoining Chloe's living quarters. Why Ross? Why not Lee? The two were as alike, physically, as brothers. Why did Ross stir that special something deep within her when for Lee she had never felt anything more than a brotherly fondness. Why? But then, why had Ross been attracted to *her* rather than to Crystal? *Or had he?* Could Crystal possibly have been right? Could it have been a case of his having taken what was offered by whichever sister came forward?

Strangely, it was this question that nagged at her through much of the remainder of the night. She'd never asked it of herself before; she'd never had cause. Now the similarities between Ross and Lee had turned her thoughts to Crystal and herself. Had it been pure chance? The simple turn of fate? But what about that coin? There had been nothing at all coincidental about Chloe winning the toss. And Ross—*had* he been looking purposely at Chloe rather than her identical twin sister? Had it been design or chance?

Her mind was clearly distracted when the men rejoined her. It was getting late. What was to happen now? Looking from one to the other, she was relieved to find that neither appeared to have a particular need for her attention at the moment. Lost in thought, she let their discussion flow around her, unaware of the looks of concern that were sent her way from alternating sources. It was Lee's voice that finally roused her.

"I'm going to run now, Chloe." He spoke from just before her chair, drawing her dark head up with a start. Taken by surprise, she straightened unsurely.

"I'm sorry, Lee," she apologized softly. "I'm afraid I haven't been much help. We haven't even gone over those things we should have—"

"No problem." He smiled. "We'll do it tomorrow." Taking his cue from the disquieted look in her eyes, he turned to Ross. "Are you staying here tonight?"

"Yes."

"No."

Both voices answered in unison. Chloe was the first to follow up. "No, Ross. You *can't* stay here!" She was determined. "There's one bedroom and one bed—and *I* need both!" *Very badly. Tonight.*

"Why don't you stay with me, friend?" Lee offered. For the second time Chloe could have disowned him— first, the invitation for dinner, now *this!* Distance was the only solution to her dilemma; Lee's offer only complicated things.

For the second time Ross accepted the other man's invitation graciously. "No imposition?"

"No way. The sofa in the living room opens into a bed. The back door will be open. Chloe will head you in the right direction." Before she could protest Lee had reached the door. "Good night, folks." He grinned, letting himself out with a flourish.

It was with a steadying breath that Chloe settled deeper into her high-backed chair, tucked her feet beneath her, forced her fingers to relax against the broad wicker arms, and looked across the room at Ross.

"You really *do* look like a princess in that chair." He spoke softly. "Those peacock feathers could as easily be a crown of gold as a swirl of wicker. Are you comfortable?" The gleam in his eye, amber and flickering, held his subtle mockery.

"No," she answered honestly. "You know I'm not."

His grin held no apology. "That's a shame. I don't want you to be miserable through the entire weekend."

"You can't stay all weekend!"

"And why not? You've just heard for yourself that I have a place to sleep. That Lee is a good fellow."

"Hah! *Too* good!" she grumped. "And I thought I could trust him."

Ross ignored her pointed comment. "That's what puzzles me." He sat forward, forearms resting on his thighs, fingers steepled. "I'm sure you *can* trust him, but I can't figure out for the life of me why."

It was one thing for Chloe to criticize her friend, totally another for Ross to do so. She was quick to come to Lee's defense. "What do you mean by that, Ross? Lee has been a true friend to me."

"That's just it." The deep voice rolled smoothly. "Why only a true friend? Why not a lover?"

"Lee doesn't want that from a woman."

"You mean, he prefers—"

"No! You twist things!" Beneath his stare, her own insides twisted. "Lee was married once. He has two children. He and his wife divorced five years ago—she lives in St. Louis now."

Ross nodded. "Burned once . . . okay, I'll accept that."

"How kind," she murmured beneath her breath. "But what about you, Ross? In the eleven years since *I knew you when,* what have *you* done along similar lines?" The source of her boldness was a mystery to her, yet she barreled on, perhaps out of spite for his derogatory quip about Lee. "Should I assume that *you* have developed odd preferences?"

The instant she said it, she knew it had been a mistake. The dark mask that fell over Ross's features allowed nothing but amber sparks to escape. When he stood and approached her she struggled to avoid cringing more deeply into her chair. There was a satanic look about him that frightened her.

"Would that make you trust me more, Chloe?" he murmured in a voice drawn from the depths of him. He towered above her, then bent down to imprison her hands beneath his, his face within inches of hers. "I'm sorry to disappoint you, but my preferences are strictly for the opposite sex." His lips moved closer. Chloe looked down defensively, but his long body filled her range of vision. Everywhere she moved her eyes, she saw him, one point more alarming than the next. If it wasn't the vee of chest, with its wisps of dark hair edging alongside the tab of his collar, it was the solid breadth of his shoulders or the lean tapering of his rib cage or the casual set of his hips. Quickly she tore her gaze away, completely convinced of his preference. As though following her understanding, he grinned. "Any further questions?"

The slight shake of her head was enough to bring the warmth of his lips into contact with her cheek. Suddenly opposing factions attacked one another within Chloe. Pull away. Move closer. Keep your eyes shut. Look at him. Look at him. *Look at him.*

She looked. His eyes held a gentleness now, the anger of moments before having vanished. Gentleness and desire mirroring hers. So close. So far away. *Kiss me.* Don't.

He did. Very, very lightly. A ghost of a touch with shuddering intensity. Chloe's eyes were shut, her lips parted. To taste those lips once more . . .

When he kissed her again he pressed his lips against hers more positively. His tenderness brought out the crying need within her, and she moved her head closer, clung to him with her own lips, drank in the exotic tang of his mouth, so moist and strong yet soft. His tongue beckoned to hers, luring it for a brief touch before he raised his head.

"Very definitely my preference." He spoke thickly, his chest rapidly rising and falling beneath her clouded gaze.

Chloe floundered in a momentary sea of disorientation before reality returned, gathering and crashing in on her.

"What am I doing?" she whispered, not realizing she'd spoken aloud. *"What am I doing?"*

"You're letting yourself live, Chloe," came the husky but gentle declaration.

"No . . . no . . ." Burying her face in her hands, she struggled to understand what had just happened. Unable to face him, much less herself, she pressed her fingers angrily against her forehead. The silken cascade of hair fell forward past her cheeks, shielding her, however thinly, from the world. What had she done? How *could* she have fallen so quickly from firm resolve? Would it always be this way—with Ross?

In the silence of her self-reproach Chloe was unaware that he had moved away, back toward the sofa from which he'd originally uncoiled. He was waiting, listening, when she finally spoke. Her face was pale as she lifted it from hiding, her eyes dark and haunted.

"Why are you doing this to me?" she pleaded softly. "Why can't you just leave me alone?"

There was a glimmer of puzzlement in his own gaze. "I've spent a good deal of time asking myself a similar question these past two weeks." He paused to study his clenched knuckles before continuing. "All I can say is that, for the first time in years, *I care.*"

He seemed to be wrestling an unseen foe, which penetrated her wall of self-disdain to spur her on. "What do you mean, Ross?" she asked falteringly.

"You asked me what I've done with myself during the past years. Well"—his snort held its own share of disgust—"I'm afraid to say I haven't been quite as noble as you. There have been many women over the years."

She had assumed as much and felt no resentment. There was a certain solace in the knowledge that, even with such a history, he was still attracted to her. After all, he *was* magnificent. Many women must have tried to tie him down.

"You found no one special?" she asked quietly.

Ross was just as quiet. "Some I liked more than others. But, no, there was no one special. No one who meant enough to tempt me to change my life-style." At her frown of bemusement, he explained. "I travel constantly. I do own an old brownstone in Manhattan, but I doubt if I spend a total of three months a year there. Hotel rooms, friends' apartments, rented suites—that's been home for the past few years."

"It's served your purpose."

"Yes." His eyes held tightly to hers, tearing into her heart. With their amber force he said much more, all silent, all mindbending. For a fleeting instant's insanity she wanted . . . she wanted . . . What *did* she want?

Ross took in her even white teeth worrying the lower lip he had teased moments earlier. His sigh was one of resignation. "I *am* a successful businessman." It was a statement of fact, devoid of arrogance. "But that's not enough."

His train of thought was all too clear to her. "I can't help you on that score, Ross." She shook her head determinedly.

"Can't . . . ?" Semantics again?

"Won't! If it's a wife and a family you want, a home in the country, perhaps a few dogs and horses, even sheep, you'll have to look elsewhere. I can't be anything but what I am at this very minute."

His voice hit a dangerously low note. "I never mentioned those things, Chloe. Are those things that *you* wanted once? Haven't you ever wished for a husband who loves you, children, pets, friends, property? What is it *you* want from life?"

"I want just what I've got now. I don't want to look back and I won't look ahead. The life I've built for myself is one in which I feel perfectly at ease. I'm content."

"Are you?" he challenged. "Don't you ever stop to wonder what it might have been like if—"

"That's enough!" Chloe exploded, jumping to her feet. "I didn't ask you to come here, Ross. I didn't ask you to stay. As of this very moment"—her stiffened finger pointed to the floor for emphasis—"I don't care *what* you do! Stay as long as you want—but don't expect to change the way I see the world. I've done quite well on my own for the past eleven years—I intend to do so for a good while longer!" Realizing that her hand was shaking, she quickly jammed it into the back pocket of her jeans. "I'm going to bed. You can see yourself out!" With a whirl that sent her hair flaring out behind, she stormed from the room, ran up the stairs, and firmly closed the door to her room behind her.

Trembling uncontrollably now, she collapsed onto the bed to stare silently at the ceiling. Her ragged breathing was the only sound that broke the night's quiet, the only sound that muffled the opening and closing of the front door as Ross left the house.

For what seemed like hours she agonized, locked in silent battle with a horde of private ghosts. If only she had never seen Ross again. To be free, once more, of this gnawing at mind and body . . .

But she *had* seen Ross again and, according to his vow, would see more of him before he left. There was only one solution, as she saw it. She would have to steel herself to resist him. In the face of utter indifference no man in his right mind would persist. Surely then he would leave her in peace.

Was it easier said than done, though? Could she possibly be indifferent to this man who had stirred her eleven years ago, who stirred her to this moment? *She would be!* It was a vow she fully intended to keep! Her life had not been without men; Ross would simply become another. They might talk, even laugh, perhaps interact in the business sphere, but never would he penetrate the inner sanctum of her heart. No man would do that!

It was on the odd prospect of tuning Ross in to the

geological issues of the day that Chloe finally fell asleep that night. It was on a distinct note of optimism that she awoke the next morning, showered, dressed, and sailed downstairs for breakfast. It was with momentary dismay that she found her kitchen already in use—until she recalled the night's resolve, tilted up her chin, and advanced.

5

~~~~~~~~~~~~~~~

So," she mused lightly, recapturing her poise as she helped herself to a cup of the coffee he'd freshly brewed, "you've made yourself at home."

His grin was as bright as the morning sun that slanted across the porch beyond the screen. "It's a luxury and I'm thoroughly enjoying it. It's not every day that I get to putter around a cozy kitchen, much less wait on a lovely princess."

"Flattery will get you nowhere." She sighed, wishing it were so. Then, in diversion, she eyed the stove. "Bacon . . . eggs . . . home fries—you're really going to eat all *that?*"

"With your help." He nodded smugly.

"Ohhhh, no, I'm not! After a breakfast like that I'd barely be able to hold my eyes open. I've got a busy day ahead—"

"—for which you need energy. And, anyway," he called over his shoulder, undaunted as he deftly turned the bacon, "if you don't eat breakfasts like this, why such a full stock of goodies? Lee's refrigerator was bare."

"Ah-hah! So, that's it!" she exclaimed, eyes narrowing in mock suspicion. "You're starved and Lee couldn't help you out!" A helpless chuckle escaped her lips. "Lee eats out. *A lot.*"

"Here?"

She answered his question with a flip one of her own. "Do you see him here *now?*" Then she wished she hadn't said anything.

"I haven't seen him yet today. He's not upstairs, is he?"

Shaking her head, she turned toward the large bay window, whose broad seat was a favorite perch of hers. "That doesn't even deserve an answer, Ross." Sipping her coffee, she spoke absently. "As for the state of my ice box, I eat *in. A lot.* Eggs make terrific dinner omelets, bacon a great BLT, and potatoes are most definitely to be baked, then scooped, mashed with a little Parmesan cheese and cream, restuffed, dotted with butter, and broiled until delicately browned on top."

The total silence that followed her calm recitation was enough to lure her gaze back over her shoulder toward Ross. His expression was one of amusement-tinged astonishment. "That sounds fantastic! You must have memorized the cookbook."

"No. I just happen to like my potatoes that way. I make them often."

Ross leaned back against the counter, arms folded across his chest, looking absolutely predatory. "Would you make them like that for me some time—maybe with a few lamb chops, some fresh broccoli, a little wine?" he growled.

He was dangerous. A wolf ready to pounce, fresh, newly showered, clad in jeans and a black turtleneck sweater. But Chloe was determined to withstand the sensual barrage. He's just a friend, no different from Lee, she told herself, smiling with appropriate cheerfulness. "Oh, I make a meal of the potatoes. If you'd like to do up the rest, be my guest." With a shrug, she slid down onto the window seat and looked toward the beach. "It's a beautiful day again!"

"Uh-huh." His voice was muffled; he must have turned back to his cooking. *Good.* A self-satisfied smile curved her lips, prompting his instant response. "You're looking particularly pleased this morning." So he *had* been watching after all. "Sleep well?"

"Not bad." Once she had fallen asleep. "How about you?" Looking back, she caught the warmth of his gaze for an instant before he turned to reach for plates from the cupboard.

"About the same."

It was an odd choice of words, she mused, unless he saw through her guise. But his face was hidden now; all that was left to her view was his back. *All?* There was a full head of thick and vibrant dark hair, damp and alive, a torso whose manly lines were shown off to perfection by the snug fit of his sweater, a pair of lean hips and long, sturdy legs, not to mention well-worn leather boots. Had he done it on purpose? She stiffened, then forced herself to take a deep breath. *Let him!* If it was the past he sought, she would take that in stride as well!

"All set?" With a knowing grin he placed two brimming plates on the table. Then, following her line of vision and noting her subsequent dismay, he added a gentle, "Don't worry, Chloe. Whatever you can't finish, I will."

Pushing herself from her perch with a skeptical grimace, she joined him. "You'd better get started then," she quipped pertly. "I'm nearly finished." Her drained coffee cup was offered up in explanation. "This is all I usually have, with a slice of toast or a muffin." Nonetheless, she took a seat opposite him, aware of his close scrutiny as she eased herself down, yet totally unprepared for his inquiry. When he made it, she nearly choked on her egg.

"Do the people you work with know about your past?"

Her silver gaze flew sharply to his before it mellowed into a more haunted look as she smiled wanly. "You make it sound lurid." Her gaze fell to her fork as she pushed home fries around her plate. "They know where I come from—some even know that I had a sister. Lee knows most of the story. But the lovely thing about this life, I've found, is that my friends and business associates see me for what I am today. It's much easier not having to constantly contend with the past."

Ross was puzzled. His dark brows met as he frowned. "Why do you assume that you'd have to do that anywhere? It's been eleven years, Chloe. The world goes on. People accept change. You seem to be the only one who can't move on."

Chloe's fork fell from her suddenly shaking hand and hit the china plate. "I look in the mirror every morning. How can I forget? How can my family forget? How can those people we knew as kids forget, when they see Crystal in my face?" She stood up unsurely. "And besides, is it right to forget? Crystal was my sister. More than that . . ." Suddenly, she could say no more. Turning her back on Ross, she walked slowly to the window. The sight of the surf rolling gracefully onto the beach calmed her.

"I'm really not like this," she murmured softly, speaking to herself as much as to him. "Morbidity isn't my style. I loved Crystal. She was my twin. Very few people can begin to understand what it meant to me to lose her."

"Perhaps that's because you don't share your feelings very often." His voice was close behind her. As he spoke she felt the warmth of his body reaching out to comfort her. When he slid his arms around her waist and drew her back against his tall, sheltering form she did not resist. His support was infinitely reassuring.

"And I don't know exactly why I'm doing it now," she whispered. "Maybe it's because you've come out of that past to haunt me." Of her own will, she turned in the circle of his arms to face him. Tipping her head up, she studied the strong features above her. "Is that what you've done—come to haunt me?"

"No, Chloe." There was a sadness in his brief smile, intermingled with a tenderness she savored. "I told you yesterday that I want to go forward, not back. I'm beginning to wonder about *you*, though. You may *have* to go back, to resolve all those things in your mind, before you can move forward."

"But I've done so well up until now," she protested. Without thinking twice, she had lifted her hands to his chest, where they lay quite comfortably, absorbing his strength.

"Of course you have, Chloe. But perhaps it was inevitable that at some point something would happen to make you face whatever it is that haunts you so."

"It's not that bad."

"No?"

It was all he had to say. There was no censure in his tone, no pity in his gaze. It was as though he knew more about her than she knew about herself. His hands left her back to stroke her cheeks for a fleeting moment before he stepped away from her. An exaggerated sigh lifted his broad shoulders; his dark head angled toward the forgotten breakfast.

"I'd better get this cleaned up. You have to get to work."

For long moments Chloe stood rooted to the floor. Puzzled, she followed his movements from table to sink, then back and forth once more. He had been so warm, so gentle, so understanding. He had been so close, yet he hadn't tried to kiss her. There had been no repeat of the impassioned lovemaking they'd shared once. But there *was* something. *Something.* As she finally headed for the door, bound for her office, she wondered about it.

"Chloe?" Her head shot up and around. Ross stood tall near her, his arm extended. "Here's a fresh cup. Why don't you take it with you?"

She did take it with her, and it helped—both the warming brew and the thoughtfulness behind it.

Once settled in her office, she was safe, firmly rooted in the present. There were reports to read, studies to review, proposals to consider. The more she worked, the better she felt. For the first time since having done the lab work earlier that week she was able to reflect on the sediment analysis of samples taken along an increasingly unstable portion of the Cape Cod National Seashore.

"Problems?" Debbie Walker popped her head in shortly after eleven.

"Oh, hi, Deb! Come on in." She smiled, erasing the puckering of her brow to welcome her petite, sandy-haired associate. "It's that Cape analysis. I was just studying the results of the work I did last week. I've got the grain sizes of the sand pretty much divided by sections. Boy, they've really botched it!"

" 'They' being the people who put that parking lot so close to the cliff?"

Chloe sighed. "You got it! It's begun to erode already, and the locals want to sue. According to my initial calculations, they've got a case."

"Will you be called in to testify?"

"I'm not sure. I've got to work this report up into some kind of written form. Depending on what happens when they read it, whether or not the matter can be settled first, it may not make it into court." Sitting back in her chair, she shook her head sadly. "You know, it's a shame that we seem to learn things *after* the fact. If only those large development corporations had gotten a geologist to advise them at the start!"

Debbie smiled. "You make a great crusader. I wish I could present *my* case as well as you do."

"And I wish *I* could handle those computers as well as *you* do," Chloe quipped in return. "But, come on—let's take a look at your statistics."

They spent the next half hour reviewing the work Debbie had done. Between them, they formulated a plan of attack both on the sinkhole in question and the people in a position to do something about it. Suitably buoyed, and with her work cut out for her, Debbie left, to be replaced moments later by a slightly groggy-looking Josh Anderson.

"How's it going, Josh?" Chloe grinned. "Late night last night?"

"Don't you know it, Chloe," came the murmured reply. "But I wanted to discuss this curriculum guide with you. If the preliminaries are all right, I'd like to work out more of the details."

Chloe's arched brow spoke volumes, as did the slow perusal she gave the casually disheveled graduate student. "You sure you're up to it?" With great effort she stifled a broader grin. Josh was a favorite of hers. Several years her junior, he was working toward his degree at Brown. This was his second year as a part-time employee of ESE.

His proposed high school geology curriculum was as fine as any she could have hoped ESE would produce.

Now he lowered his voice in conspiracy. "I'd *really* be up to it if I could take a swig of the coffee that smells so good in there." He quirked his head toward the kitchen.

"Why don't you?"

"It's that watchdog . . ." Still his tone was ultralow.

"Watchdog?"

"You know—that tall guy out there. The dark one in the living room. He doesn't seem to appreciate the traffic in here. Who is he, anyway? And what's he doing in *our* house?"

For the better part of the morning Chloe had forced all thoughts of Ross from her mind. Now, revived by the work that she loved, she was able to chuckle at Josh's reference.

"He's a friend," she answered simply.

"You're sure about that?"

"I'm sure. Go on out and get your coffee. If he starts to snarl, you can send him in here."

Josh's face took on a dubious I-hope-you-know-what-you're-doing-lady look. Nonetheless, he pulled himself up to his full five-foot-seven height, squared his shoulders, and made as grand an exit as was possible for someone going to face the proverbial giant. With a helpless grin Chloe sat back in her chair, elbows on its arms, fingers comfortably intertwined.

So Ross had decided to spend the morning in her living room. What was he doing there? Was he bored? Impatient? Annoyed that she was carrying on as usual? *Good!*

"You wanted to see me?" His deep voice rumbled in resonant waves from the door, across the room, and into Chloe's ears with startling clarity.

"Who, *me?*"

His gaze scanned the room. "I don't see anyone else in here . . . for a change. They may not actually *live* here, but they run in and out all day, don't they?"

"It's an open office, you might say."

"I do say. Say, when are you going to be done?"

"Done?" she echoed innocently, then gestured toward the desktop with feigned bewilderment. "Lord knows! I've got two reports to look through yet. And Josh will be back any—There he is!" His timing was perfect. "Josh, meet Ross." As the two shook hands, Chloe stared helplessly at the appalling discrepancy in their heights.

No wonder Josh had been intimidated; not only did Ross tower over him, but their respective physiques were about as alike as night and day. A spontaneous protectiveness surged within her.

"Why don't you sit down, Josh? Ross, would you excuse us? We'll be a little while."

"I'll be waiting." He smiled, then turned and left.

Josh was far from thick. "Listen, Chloe, are you sure you wouldn't rather go over this another time?"

"What?" she ribbed him gently. "And waste the effort it took for you to pull yourself out of bed? Carry on!"

It was a full hour later when Josh finally left. Chloe walked him to the door and had an instant to note that Ross was occupied with a briefcase of his own before greeting Lee, who bounded through the living room to deliver a wave in passing to Ross, then looped an arm about Chloe's waist and corraled her in her office once more.

"It's about time you're free," he broke out in good-humored chiding. "You're a busy lady!"

Chloe smiled affectionately. "Well, I'm all yours now. I want to show you—"

"Wait." He held a hand up to forestall her. "There's something we'd better discuss first." Her eyes widened expectantly. "I think"—he enunciated each word carefully—"that we may have a problem." He paused.

"A problem?" Tensing, she forced an apprehensive grin. "Come on, Lee. You know I can't stand suspense."

Eyeing her warily, he yielded. "I had two cancellations yesterday."

"Cancellations?"

"That's right. The schools. They simply don't have the money to finance us for the next semester."

"That's terrible!" Chloe exclaimed. "I just sent Josh out of here with a fantastic proposal. Do you mean to say that he won't be able to apply it?"

Lee shook his head. "Not in Hingham or Westerly he won't. There are still the wealthier communities . . ." His voice trailed off, his further implication clear.

"But not for long. That's it, isn't it? You think we're headed down a dead-end street?"

"Unfortunately, unless something dramatic happens with the economy, yes."

She thought aloud, voicing her partner's sentiment. "And, since a good third of our work is through the public schools, we'd better branch out ourselves, is that it?"

"Smart girl."

"Private enterprise," she announced without hesitation.

"Come again? Business isn't our field."

Chloe laughed at the look of confusion on Lee's bearded face. "No, it certainly isn't. But I said it to Debbie earlier this morning and I meant it. What we need is to affiliate ourselves with corporations as resident geologists, be the geologists-on-call for several of these large development corporations. You know, like—"

"—like the Hansen Corporation?"

The thought took her completely off-guard. "No! That was the last thing I had in mind! I was thinking more of firms like Cabot and Walker, or Fennimen East."

Lee smiled smugly. "What's wrong with the Hansen Corporation?"

"What's wrong—" She caught herself and abruptly lowered her voice. "What's wrong with the Hansen Corporation is that Ross Stephenson is its president!"

"So?"

"Lee," she pleaded, "Ross is a friend. I would no more ask him to hire ESE than . . . than . . ." At a loss for words, she groped helplessly. It was bad enough that Ross was here on her doorstep for the weekend. Whatever would happen if she had to *work* with the man?

Lee grew suddenly more serious. "What is he to you, Chloe?"

She sighed, giving up the struggle to find excuses. "He's a . . . friend. We knew each other before . . . before Crystal died."

"He's the one, isn't he?" There was only kindness in Lee's voice, yet his words jolted her.

"What?" she whispered falteringly.

"He's the one—the man in your life."

"There is no man in my life, Lee. You know that."

Lee too was familiar with the haunted cast that occasionally entered Chloe's eyes. He saw it now and grew more gentle. "Over the years I've learned a lot about you. You've told me about your sister, that she died, that you rarely go home to your family back in New Orleans. But you never talk of men. You're a beautiful person, Chloe. I know it and *he* knows it." He tilted his head toward the living room, where Ross was apparently engrossed in whatever it was that he had in his briefcase. "I dare you to look me in the eye and deny that there was ever anything between the two of you."

Strangely, she had no desire to lie. "I can't do that, Lee. But, whatever it was, it's over."

"You think so?"

"Yes!"

His contemplation of her lasted but a minute longer. In a flurry of movement, he wiped his hands together. "Well, then, I guess that settles that." Nothing had been settled; they both knew it. But Lee wisely redirected the conversation onto safer ground. "I do agree with you that the private business sector would be a promising outlet to tap. I'll be going to Washington next week to work with the Coast Guard on their Gulf project. I'll see what nosing around I can do while I'm there."

"How much longer will the training project take?"

"With the government, that's a good question. And

when it comes to oil spill cleanups, no amount of training is ever enough. I would guess, though, that the present phase will take another few months at least."

Nodding silently, Chloe contemplated those coming few months. Then, unthinkingly, she glanced toward the door.

Lee bounded up. "I can take the hint, pretty lady." His hand was on the knob before she could call him back. "Anything further will wait. Have fun!" His departing wink held a bundle of mischief.

"Lee! Wait—"

One dark head disappeared to make way for another. "At last!" Ross exclaimed. He smartly closed the office door. "*Alone . . . at last!*"

Chloe forced herself to sit back slowly. "I hope you were able to find something to do. I had no idea you'd stick around *all* morning."

"Actually"—he circled her desk to plant himself on the corner nearest her—"I was able to go over some papers of my own. I'm a good loser . . . for a morning." He paused and looked toward the door. "Shall we go?"

"Go? Where?"

"Oh"—he looked out the window in amusement—"I thought you could show me around town. I *am* a stranger to these parts."

Judging from the air of supreme confidence he exuded, it was a wonder that *any* parts were strange to him. Chloe couldn't ignore the thread of excitement he seemed to have brought with him into the room. Without a doubt, Ross Stephenson was far too dangerous to be borne at such close range.

Standing quickly, she tried to remedy the situation. "I don't know, Ross. I still have—" A strong arm snagged her around the waist and he imprisoned her between his thighs.

"Oh, no, you don't! All work and no play—"

"Makes a successful scientist—"

"And a very dull woman."

She frowned, unwittingly nibbling at his bait. "You don't think my work is dull, do you?" Her disappointment was genuine, as was the devastatingly handsome smile that spread slowly across his face. His hands, looped loosely behind her back, brought her closer.

"*Nothing* about you is dull, Chloe," he crooned, "except, of course, your determination to hold me at arms' length."

Arms' length was a lot further than where she was now. Well within the circle of his arms, her hands having fallen to the point where his jeans met his hips, she was under his spell once more.

Ross lowered his head and kissed her, tasting the sweetness of her mouth, a gift she was powerless at that moment to withhold. Perhaps, she was later to muse, she had been too successful at her own game. By denying the fact that Ross meant anything more to her than as a stranger who had walked into her home the day before, she responded to him simply as a man whose virile appeal stirred her.

Her return kiss was gentle, sampling. She played with being free, being free of all memory, all guilt. Her lips opened to his, and she gave of herself as she hadn't done in years. It was as though Ross pulled something from the most private depths of her that satisfied them both.

"That was nice," he whispered against her lips, then pulled away and set her back before she moved herself. He trailed a long forefinger across her cheek to the lips he'd just left. "We'll do it again soon."

It was said so gently and carried such lightness that Chloe couldn't help but smile. A warm flush painted her cheeks a comely pink, complementing the gray of her eyes, which held a hint of apology. "You have this way of sneaking up when a girl least expects it, Ross. What am I going to do with you?" she whispered.

His gaze sent silent messages of manly intent echoing

through her utter femininity. "You're going to love me one day. *That's* what you're going to do." As she stiffened, he went quickly on. "But right now you're going for a ride with me."

"I have errands to do . . ." she protested feebly.

"Like . . . ?"

"Like the marketing, for one thing. In one meal you've practically wiped me out!"

"Then we'll go to the market. What else?"

She improvised. "I was hoping to pick up some new houseplants to hang in the living room. With winter coming on—"

"Winter? It's creeping up toward seventy again today. How can you think of winter?"

"It'll be here. And anyway, the sooner the plants get used to the house, the easier it will be for them to adapt to the cooler weather."

His gaze narrowed. "I bet you talk to your plants, too."

"No." She smiled softly, all too aware of amber eyes seemingly glued to her lips as she spoke. "If I did *that,* they might think I was a little off balance. If nothing else I want my plants to respect me!"

It was doubtful that Ross heard her last quip. A state of hypnosis seemed to have come over him. Suddenly he slid the fingers of both hands through the hair on either side of her face, brought his own head down, and kissed her again. This time there was a hunger there hadn't been before. This time there was a new urgency. This time Chloe was frightened. It would be so simple to lose herself in that hunger, to share it, to sate it.

"Ross!" she cried. "Please, don't!"

At the high pitch of her voice he released her instantly. Could he know of her own frustration? she wondered. Could he sense that her fear was of herself?

"Okay, Chloe." He spoke softly, a husky note in his voice. "I won't push you now. But you will love me one day. One day soon."

"You're wrong—" she began in a whisper, only to be interrupted.

"Not this time, princess." Then he paused as his breathing grew steadier, offering Chloe precious time to do the same. "Let's go. We'll stop for lunch first. I'm starved!"

"After that breakfast?"

"That breakfast," he growled playfully, "was interrupted, as I recall. And anyway, that was this morning. It's nearly two. Have you got any other feeble excuses to try on me before we leave?"

Chloe looked around her office, its familiarity giving her strength to face the strange situation in which she found herself. Determined once again to prove her immunity through action, despite the momentary setback she'd just suffered, she drew in a deep breath. "Not a one," she declared pertly, preceding Ross from the room without another word. It was only when they had reached the front door that an odd sense of adventure surged through her. Eyes alight, she turned back toward the tall, dark potentate who followed. "I've got a great idea! Let's take the bike!"

"I've got a better idea," Ross countered. "Let's get changed into cooler things. I hadn't counted on a recurrence of this heat when I dressed this morning."

Assuming that his clothes were still at Lee's house, she felt particularly generous. "Why don't you go back and change? I'll just sit here and—wait! What do you think you're doing?"

There was no question as to what he was doing. With an unceremonious tug he freed his sweater from the confines of his jeans, crisscrossed his arms over his ribs, and smoothly whipped the black turtleneck over his head and off. Never, ever, would Chloe forget that moment when, muscles stretched, his chest came into view.

Lightly bronzed and bearing a liberal hazing of hair that tapered wickedly toward his navel, it was a solid wall of hard, manly flesh, muscled and glorious. Her mouth suddenly dry, she could only stare.

"My bags are right here," came the maddeningly nonchalant reply, as the splendid male before her bent to retrieve a soft leather duffel from beside the sofa. Long arms released the zipper and deft fingers exchanged the sweater for a lighter-weight, short-sleeved jersey. With a swift movement he drew it over his head. Once more Chloe trembled as that body stretched, flexed, then settled back down to its natural imposing state, mercifully covered again.

"There." Ross grinned. Could he actually read her mind? She wondered. "That was easy enough. Are *you* cool enough?"

Cool seemed an impossibility. "Uh, I'm fine." She cleared her throat awkwardly, turning and escaping to the wide-open spaces without any further attempt at wit. She moaned inwardly. And she had suggested taking the bike! Better that they should swim; they might not get to any store, but they would certainly have a barrel of much-needed cold water between them!

But . . . too late. He was at her heels as she led the way to the side shed that housed her motorbike.

"You drive this yourself?" Ross asked, eyeing the small vehicle with something short of trust.

"Sure," she laughed, praying that he not hear her faint breathlessness and guess its cause. "It's great for the fresh air, uses practically no gas, and does much less by way of pollution than my car. Unless"—she paused teasingly—"you'd feel safer—"

"No way! I'm game. Don't forget—*I'm* the original hippie of the pair."

Chloe drove with Ross straddling the seat behind her. It was every bit as traumatic as she had imagined it would be. He was near, so near. His arms were locked about her waist, tucking her body back against his. Even the early October breeze did nothing to relieve the intimacy of the trip. When he spoke, it was a nibble at her ear. *A nibble?* Had he *really* done that—or was it a product of her overworked imagination? She no longer knew.

The road they traveled was one she covered daily. Its sides were edged with maples and oaks, grown ripe and mellow now, on the verge of bursting into the vivid flames of autumn. Fields sprawled to the right, wooded pastureland to the left. Ahead undulated a path to Sakonnet Point, on the tip of the finger of land on which Little Compton sat just across the bay from Newport.

If Ross was aware of the havoc his nearness wreaked on her, he kept his smugness in check. Once, in a gesture laden with soft intimacy, he released her waist to gather her long flow of hair together in his hands, twist the fall once, and tuck it safely inside the back of her shirt.

"The better to see the town," he murmured wickedly, for he had to know that her neck tingled from the touch of those fingers in transit, her ear from the brush of his breath, so much so that she was oblivious to much of their surroundings. When at last they reached the wharf, with its graceful fleet of pleasure craft, Chloe was strangely torn. But not so Ross.

"Ah! There's a place that looks like it will fit the bill! Can we get a bite to eat there?"

It was the ultimate humiliation—to be bested by a restaurant. Had Ross been *totally* immune to the sensual force that had shaken her for the past ten minutes? It seemed, she mused, that the way to a man's heart *was* through his stomach after all. But then she caught herself again. *She* wanted no part of Ross's heart. Let the restaurant have him!

"Sure can." She smiled, pleased to have pulled herself so neatly from his web. "If you're really hungry, this is the place."

Ross *was* really hungry. He was game to sample most

anything and everything, from quahaug, or clam, fritters to little necks on the half shell to swordfish puffs, a specialty of the house.

Chloe savored his enthusiasm, taking pride in pointing out the small groups of local fishermen on the pier arduously scraping barnacles off tall-stacked lobster traps. The bright yellow of their rubber overalls was a bit of sunshine stolen from the sky to spark life into the otherwise sleepy air of the harbor. It was, all in all, a peaceful lunch, filled with good food, thirst-quenching beer, and conversation that stuck to the more general, less personal topic of travels, foreign ports, and favorite hideaways.

"The ocean is beautiful," Ross admitted at one point, "but I think I still prefer the mountains. There's nothing more lovely than that feeling of seclusion you get in a small cabin tucked into a neat cleft, with stretches and stretches of piggybacked hills to keep the world at bay."

"Then *you've* never been on the beach on a foggy morning," Chloe countered softly. "It's like being in a gentle white cocoon, with the solace of knowing that humanity is near, yet out of sight and sound for as long as the mist should choose."

"You like New England, don't you?"

"I do."

"You'll be staying here?"

"I will."

"Then," he sighed, reluctant to break the rapport they had established, "we'd better get you to the market or you won't make it through the week, much less the winter."

It was on that comfortable note that they left the restaurant, spending leisurely moments wandering along the breakwater before returning to the bike.

"*I'll* drive this time." Ross lifted a dark brow, holding a palm out for the keys. Chloe was only too glad to relinquish the responsibility—and with just reason. For, seated comfortably *behind* Ross, she was more in control of her emotions. What she hadn't counted on was the broad expanse of his back, the sense of contentment that flowed through her as the wind now rushed freely through her hair, the gentle fatigue that a night of little sleep, a morning of busy work, and a full stomach could so easily induce. The temptation was simply too great. Without a care to the wisdom of the move she wrapped her arms about his middle and laid her cheek flush against his back. It was heaven, pure and simple. She had not a care in the world; all would be watched over by the tall, dark master at the controls. Above the wind that sailed by as they cut cleanly through it came the steady beat of his heart, giving her strength. What it was about the man—this particular man—that so profoundly affected her, she didn't know, nor did she care to ponder, at the moment. It was enough to enjoy the respite from responsibility and to give herself up to his care, if only for the brief trip home.

The brief trip home, however, grew strangely long. Peering from behind Ross's back, Chloe saw that they were on a road they had not traveled earlier.

"Do you know where we are?" she yelled.

"Sure! I've got a great sense of direction. Where is your market?"

He followed her pointing finger, turning this way, then that, until the town common came into view. Typically New England, it had a white-steepled church at its hub and a variety of rural shops and boutiques. Chloe found everything she needed at the grocery store, reluctantly took Ross's suggestion that the plants be saved for another trip, then climbed behind him onto the bike once more to return to the house. True to his word, his sense of direction *was* good. Not one wrong turn later she found herself on her own front steps.

With the moment of reckoning at hand, she felt maddeningly hesitant. "Will you . . . be . . . returning to New York now?"

He had finished stowing the bike in its proper spot and advanced on her with a grin, giving her a moment's fright before he gallantly relieved her of the large brown bag she'd been carrying and, taking her elbow, propelled her toward the house. There was mischief in his eyes. "Not yet."

"You're going back to Lee's?"

Deliberately, he shook his head. "Not yet."

"Then"—unsureness made her bold—"what *do* you plan to do?"

He held the door open for her to pass, then followed her and went directly to the kitchen, where he quite comfortably began to unload and store the groceries. "I plan to make several phone calls"—pausing to glance at his watch, he nodded in satisfaction at the time—"then wash the car, catch the end of the Giants' game, shower and shave, and take you out to dinner."

His recitation had been so nonchalant that Chloe would have surmised this to be the precise way Ross spent every Saturday in October. Perhaps, she mused then, the first part was; as for taking her out to dinner, *that* had never happened before.

"It's unnecessary, Ross—"

"Which part," he interrupted boyishly, "the calls, the car, the game, or the shower?"

"The *dinner!*" He'd purposely left that out! "Lunch was enough to even us up. There's no need for anything further."

A muscle working overtime in Ross's jaw was the only sign of the tension that flitted momentarily through him. "It's not tit-for-tat, Chloe. I would *like* to take you out to dinner."

"I appreciate the thought, Ross, but—"

"No buts about it! You're coming to dinner with me, and that's all there is to it!"

"What if I already have plans?"

He quirked a dark brow. "Do you?"

"I could just as well," she hedged, "for the way *you* simply assume I'm free."

"Well . . . are you?"

Her sigh was one of resignation. "Yes." It wasn't that she didn't want to go to dinner with Ross. On the contrary. His company was far too pleasant! It would be all too easy to grow used to his presence, and *that* she could never do!

"Good. Say, about eight?"

"But—"

"Uhhhh . . ." His rich baritone crooned its warning. "Eight it is. And, Chloe?"

Her feeling of total helplessness was echoed in her voice. "Yes?"

"How about if we dress up?"

"Dress up? I haven't 'dressed up' in months! Things here are very casual. There's nowhere—"

"You leave that to me," he argued gently.

Chloe lowered her eyes and studied the floor, then slowly shook her head as awareness dawned. "Ross," she sighed, protesting now in a near-whisper, "I'd really rather—"

"For old times' sake, Chloe," he dared to murmur. "Today we played 'far out.' Tonight, let's play 'far in.' Come on. How about it? Just this once?"

The odd note of pleading in his voice brought Chloe's head slowly up. His face bore such an expression of innocence, of hope, that she could not have turned him down.

"Just this once," she acquiesced softly, forcing the semblance of a smile to lips that were warm and vulnerable.

There was, however, no "semblance" whatsoever in Ross's smile. It was broad and open, relieved and pleased. It penetrated her wall of hesitancy to scatter excitement into every corner of her being. It warmed her, reassured her, amused her. And it most definitely excited her. For that reason she was terrified!

"It's a date!" he exclaimed with determination, then turned and headed for the phone, leaving Chloe to gather the pieces of her fast-splintering resolve and struggle with makeshift repairs before evening rolled around.

6

It wasn't an easy task, for Ross seemed to be everywhere she turned. He invaded her office to make his calls, lounging back in her chair, legs long and straight, crossed lazily at the ankles, propped on the corner of her desk. His presence filled the room so that it took a conscious effort on Chloe's part to quietly creep in and steal her own work. His eyes openly followed her every move, though he was maddeningly capable of participating, when the party at the distant end of the wire demanded it, in what was obviously a business discussion.

After retreating to the back porch to bask in the rays of the westward sun, she put her best effort into organizing the papers on her lap. Her best effort was, however, sadly lacking. As though conjured up by her preoccupation, Ross appeared soon after to inquire about a bucket, a sponge, and some old towels. He was right on schedule, his self-satisfied air announced. He vanished, then reappeared. The tools of his momentary trade, collected from diverse parts indicated by Chloe, were deposited on the sandy grass adjacent to the very same porch on which she sat. Would he? She wondered. The smooth hum of his car's engine as he pulled the vehicle close by the side of the house gave her her answer. So he wanted an audience. It was a deliberate ploy to distract her . . . again.

Glued to her large wood-slatted porch chair, Chloe couldn't seem to move. Her gaze held on Ross as he put his best effort into washing, drying, and polishing his sporty brown BMW. As he stretched to soap the roof, the muscles of his shoulders bunched. When he squatted to scrub the whitewalls, the muscles of his thighs swelled. The span of the front windshield demanded enough of a reach to free his shirt from his jeans, thereby serving up fleeting, devastating glimpses of a flat, hard belly. And through it all was the sight of hands and forearms at work, lightly tanned, softly haired, twisted tautly with sinewed strength.

When Chloe had taken about as much as she could without risking the total loss of her sensual control, she stacked her papers into a random pile, bounded from the chair, and, without a word to explain her abrupt departure, vanished into the house. To clean? *She hated to clean!* Yet it seemed one way to expend a portion of the nervous energy that had gathered deep within her.

She swept the floors and vacuumed the carpets, all at doublespeed, all with every bit of elbow grease she could muster. Tables, chairs, countertops, and shelves met similar fates at the hand of her dustcloth. Perspiration beaded on her upper lip; in frustration, she brushed it away. *Damn him for his virility!* Sprawled at her desk . . . draped across the car—what next?

Next was the football game. It was a different torment this time, but one that was no less agonizing. She was deeply engrossed in polishing the aged oak banister halfway to the second floor when the familiar sound wafted up to her, and she crumbled down on the homey wool runner in defeat. The football game—what memories it brought back. That sound—the constantly excited roar of the crowd, with the babble of the color commentators, the endless streams of kickoffs and passes, punts and first downs, fumbles, tumbles, and pile-ups—brought back the days in New Orleans when the men of the family would gather for their weekly fix. Her brothers—it had been so long since she'd seen them— Were they watching this game as well? And her father— how was he feeling? He wasn't as young now as he'd been then. Should she make that supreme effort to go back before . . . before . . .

"Are you all right, Chloe?"

It wasn't until Ross had spoken that she realized he'd even approached. Nor had she been aware of the tears that had gathered behind her eyes. With a hard swallow and a feeble smile, she willed away the sadness. "Yes. I'm fine. I . . . uh . . . I think I'll run for a while. The exercise would be therapeutic."

Leaving Ross where he stood looking up at her, one hand on the banister, the other in his pocket, she turned and pensively covered the last of the steps to the top landing, disappeared into her room to change into shorts and a T-shirt, then retraced her route.

Her sneaker-clad feet beat a rhythmic path down the beach toward the far end of the bay, much as they had done at roughly the same time the day before. Had it only been twenty-four hours since Ross had shown up? Already he seemed so at home here. Moreover, it seemed so natural to *have* him here.

The spate of questions kept apace with her jog. Was it only that Ross was a figure from her past? Did he remind her of her home—*that* home? Of her family? Of her father and brothers? Was he a link to those people who

had once meant—who still did mean, if she faced the
truth—so very much to her? Much as she wished to deny
it, did she crave the warmth of family? Was Ross, by
association, an extension of them? Was that in part
responsible for his appeal?

Stymied in her search for answers, she paced herself
for another ten minutes before finally turning to back-
track. When she reached the house she didn't bother to
stop at the door. Her momentum carried her into the
kitchen at an easy lope, through to the living room, then
up the stairs. No sign of Ross—so much the better.
Jogging in place with the last of her preshower energy,
she piled her arms with fresh towels from a surprisingly
low stack in the linen closet and stopped by her bedroom
for a robe. There she stopped dead in her tracks.

Where an open expanse of pale lavender quilt had
been when she'd finished making her bed that morning
was now a landscape dotted with artifacts. *Male* artifacts.
And clothes. *His* clothes. That he had made himself at
home in her house had been clear to her earlier, but *this*
was the limit!

A fit of fury took her to the bathroom door; a split
second of better judgment halted her. The sound from
within was of the sink taps running. If she barged in, what
would she find? The tremble that snaked through her
limbs at the thought had nothing to do with fear. Rather,
she conjured up the image of Ross in the act of shaving, a
coat of white lather covering his jaw, a towel—*her*
towel—covering his loins, and nothing, *nothing* else,
covering or covered.

As she stood rooted there, the sound of water ceased,
the shower curtain clattered back on its hooks,
and . . . and . . . Her mind's eye saw it all, setting her
insides aquiver. The towel, hiding so little as it was, fell
from his hips. With the nonchalance of the king of beasts,
he stepped into the shower.

Mercifully, he was unable to hear her low cry as she whirled back toward her bedroom, cursing both Ross and her very vivid imagination all the way. But she was helpless to curb her curiosity entirely. Approaching the bed with something akin to shyness, she studied his things. There was the leather duffel she had seen earlier, plus a larger, flatter suit bag, unzipped to reveal a pair of gray-blue tweed lapels. There was the much smaller canvas case that had contained his shaving gear, if the travel-sized bottle of cologne left behind were any indication. There was a shirt—white, freshly laundered, lightly starched. There were a tie, clean socks, shorts—

"Oh, Lord!" she exclaimed softly. If every stitch of the clothing he intended to put on was here on her bed, exactly *what* did he intend to wear for the trip from the bathroom?

A knot of anticipation constricted her throat, making breathing more difficult. The aftereffects of her jog had faded; this quickening was due to desire, pure and simple. The very definite awareness of a taut sensation surrounded by fire beneath her stomach spoke for itself. If only she could forget all else and give herself to this man whose unique brand of masculinity affected her as no other had. "Give herself"? That only told half the story, for at that moment Chloe knew she would take as well, take as she had been too naive to do eleven years before. She felt suddenly greedy, possessed with a need to satisfy this excruciating gnawing inside.

"You're back!"

Chloe jumped, twirling around in shock. When had his shower ended? She had heard nothing!

Undaunted by her alarm, perhaps amused at its cause, he grinned. "I had hoped to be out of your way"—he gestured in token apology toward her bed—"but I'm afraid I've misjudged the time. You beat me to it!" His gaze swung in deliberate innocence toward the hall from which he'd just come. "I hope you don't mind that I helped myself to your supplies."

The towel! *The damned towel!* Draped around his hips with as much panache—and as little ceremony—as she had earlier imagined, it hung low on his stomach and left little to the imagination. In self-defense she tore her eyes upward, following the sensual path that a line of dark and manly hair had forged. Upward to his waist, over his ribs, to his chest—she was unable to move further.

"Chloe," Ross began in husky chiding, "do you have any idea what it does to a man when a woman looks at him that way?"

It took every ounce of her willpower to keep from lowering her gaze in curiosity. Her lips felt suddenly dry and her tongue moistened them. Still her voice wobbled. "I'm sorry—"

"Oh, don't be *sorry.*" The intensity of his eyes captured hers as he stepped closer. Though he didn't touch her, his body was no more than a breath away.

The harsh gasp that escaped her lips cut him off before he could verbalize what they both knew was the truth. Her hand flew to his chest to hold him away. It was a miscalculation if ever she had made one. For her fingers discovered a mat of soft, dark hair that sprang, warm and still moist, from the freshness of his lightly bronzed skin.

The sudden pounding of her pulse threatened to deafen her, frightening her so with its force that she tore her hand from his chest and thrust it behind her back. There was a measure of guilt in her expression. His, however, reflected only the same depth of desire she felt. Amber embers smoldered freely in his gaze, heating her all the more. To forget all . . . to be held in his arms . . . to be loved. . . .

Ross lowered his head slowly, until his lips shadowed hers. She felt them, wanted them. Her own parted in silent invitation as she closed her eyes to more fully delight in the sensation. But he never kissed her. Rather, there was a soft exchange of breath, a mutual whisper of lips against one another that was sweet, sweet torment.

Chloe felt ready to burst, willing to beg. But rather than venture down that sure road to self-disgust, she finally did what she had meant to do all along. Her hands pressed against his chest, pushing him gently but firmly from her. As he slowly straightened to what was, even barefoot, an awesome height, he cleared his throat.

"You'd better wait downstairs." His voice was thick and taut, his features held in rigid control. "I'll finish up quickly."

It was his will that directed her from the bedroom and down the stairs. Sanity returned only when she reached the bottommost step. With a muttered oath she traipsed through the kitchen to the back porch overlooking the beach. But the tide within her was high; no amount of cooling breeze could stem it.

He'd have to leave; that's all there was to it! He simply couldn't stay here much longer or she would . . . she would . . . What would she do? He stirred such heart-rending sensations in her. And today he'd been cruel enough to give her a taste of what it might be like to have him around the house all the time.

Much as she tried to scowl, a surreptitious smile betrayed her innermost thoughts. It had been nice waking up to find a man in her kitchen cooking breakfast, knowing that he patiently awaited her work's end, doing such mundane chores as the marketing with him, finding him in the shower even when that had been *her* destination. It *had* been nice. But would any man fit the bill? With a sigh, she shook her head. It had to be Ross. Always Ross.

"Okay, princess. It's all yours!" came the call from the object of her thoughts.

For Chloe, grappling with her quandary, time had lost

its meaning. Now, looking up in surprise, she found the horizon boasting the pink-orange glow of imminent sunset. Looking back over her shoulder, she saw Ross in the kitchen door, the light from within silhouetting his sturdy frame.

"Be right there," she called, looking forward once more, mustering her composure, then standing to claim what was rightfully hers. The bathroom. The bedroom. What else would she be able to claim where Ross was concerned?

Gliding past him, she caught a trace of cologne, faint enough to tease with a subtlety that was intrinsically Ross. Avoiding his gaze, she moved steadily through the house until she was at last in the privacy of her room. There was no longer any sign of him, either there or in the bathroom. But in her mind—that was another matter. It was one she determinedly pushed from the fore to make way for more immediate concerns.

Promptly at eight she descended the stairs, wearing a pale blue sheath of lightweight wool appropriate to the fast-cooling night air. Its lines were simple; it was nipped in at the waist and wrists, lightly flaired at the sleeves and skirt, and deeply slashed into a vee at the throat. It was the latter that had caused her the greatest debate. In its very simplicity, the dress was provocative. She had bought it the year before for one of those "blundered" attempts at a date. Yet it was the only "dressy" dress in her wardrobe of fairly recent vintage; there had been no suitable alternative. Still she had her doubts. If only the neckline were more sedate. The last thing Ross Stephenson needed was provocation!

In other respects she felt confident. Her hair was brushed to a fine sheen, then swept back behind either ear and held in place with matching buds of pale blue silk. The single pearls of her earrings matched the long strand around her throat. The luminescence of her eyes completed the picture. She was like a porcelain princess, floating gracefully to the bottom step, and Ross was clearly pleased.

"You look lovely, Chloe," he murmured, gently taking her arm. "Are you all set?"

"Uh-huh." Fighting a strange shyness, she smiled tentatively. "Where are we going?"

"I've made reservations at Farmington Court."

"In *Newport?*"

"They don't have a Farmington Court in Little Compton, do they?" he growled playfully.

"But how did you get reservations?"

He suppressed a grin. "I managed."

Chloe's excitement was genuine. "That's fantastic! They've only had the dining room open for a few months."

"You haven't eaten there yet, have you? I was hoping I'd be the first to take you."

"You are!" she exclaimed, then tried to get a handle on her breathiness. "I told you that I usually eat in, remember? No, I haven't eaten at the Court. I understand that the dining room is as beautiful as the food is delicious." She arched a brow. "You *are* hungry, aren't you?"

Appreciating her quip, Ross smiled in return. "Since we're dining in style tonight, I'll try not to make a scene over the pâté. Come on." He cocked his head toward the door. "Let's go."

The drive to the farm took them in a large **U**, from the tip of one finger of land back to the mainland, then out to the tip of the other finger. Their conversation was light, in contrast to the heavy darkness that had fallen. Even the moon had disappeared behind the gathering clouds.

Throughout the drive, Chloe was vitally aware of Ross. His strapping presence filled the car and her senses, imbuing her with a definite sense of excitement.

Farmington Court was on the outskirts of Newport. Ross knew precisely which roads to take, puzzling Chloe.

"How did you find out about the Court, Ross?" she challenged when the farm appeared on a gentle rise ahead. "Not many people know about the dining room here. Not many outsiders, that is. It seems to be a well-kept secret."

Ross's smile reflected the bright lights of the house. "Maybe it's supposed to be a secret, but it's slowly creeping out anyway. I had a recommendation from a friend in New York who has been here." He paused for a minute, then went on. "But I have to confess that I'm not a total stranger to Newport. Little Compton, yes. Newport, no. I was here last summer."

"You were?" she asked cautiously, but her skepticism was unfounded.

He nodded. "I spent several days here, sailing with some friends."

"I didn't know you sailed."

"There's a *lot* you don't know about me." With a flick of his wrist he turned the car into a space in the graveled lot, then slid fluidly from behind the wheel and materialized at her door to help her out.

She was to learn something new about him the instant they passed through the door of the graciously sprawling seaside estate. Not only did he greet the maître d' by name, but he spoke in fluent French. Chloe remained happily silent. Not only was she reluctant to demonstrate her ignorance of the language, but she found pure pleasure in its beauty. Smooth and romantic, it was a portent of what was to come.

Following several moments of low conversation during which both men seemed equally at ease, the maître d' showed Ross and Chloe to the smallest of the three rooms that had been converted for public dining. It was exquisitely decorated in Colonial style, with a smattering of the English, a dab of the French, and a triumphant dose of pure Americana. This particular room held only three tables, each set for two. Theirs was in a far corner, lit softly by a candle. It was an intimate setting, one Chloe would have wished to avoid had she been thinking clearly.

But she wasn't. At some mysterious point Ross had ceased to be a part of the past and had commandeered her present with astonishing force. Now, in the candlelight, she looked across the linen-clothed table to meet his gaze.

"Do you like it?" he asked with subdued eagerness.

"I like it." She smiled.

"I asked the maître d' to bring a bottle of Chassagne de Montrachet."

If his fluency in French amazed her, his knowledge of fine wines was no less astonishing. Fine wines were something she *did* know something about, a legacy of her father's acclaimed cellar. Unable to resist, she dimpled into a grin. "So *that's* how the Army sedated its brats. And here I felt so sorry for you. I'm sure the Chassagne de Montrachet will be superb." The melodic twist she put on the word *superb* was as close as she could come to French.

Ross laughed. "The Army had nothing to do with it, Chloe. Actually, I developed a taste for wine after I left the Peace Corps. I have several treasured bottles at home—a Mouton-Rothschild, a Château Lafite-Rothschild. My favorite is a 1959 Côteaux du Layon from the Loire Valley."

"Whew! That's very impressive! What other goodies do you have up your sleeve?"

His right hand flew to his left cuff, one long finger making a pretense of searching. The search was forgotten, however, when the maître d' reappeared, wine in hand, to present the bottle to Ross, whose attention was instantly monopolized.

While Ross studied the wine, Chloe studied him. It was

a luxury that the drive through the night had not afforded. Now she drank in his good looks with as much reverence as he gave to his wine.

He looked superb. His suit was the same gray-blue tweed whose lapels had peered at her from her bed. His white shirt and crimson-on-navy tie were similarly familiar. She blushed as she recalled the other items she'd seen, then pushed them quickly from her mind in favor of the chiseled features before her. They were strong, yet relaxed, and exuded confidence. The darkness of his hair and the sun-touched hue of his skin contrasted with his shirt at neck and wrists, adding a crispness to his appearance that was enhanced by the fine cut of the obviously hand-tailored fabric. He was the epitome of the man of the world—suave, assured, experienced, and content. To all outward appearances he held the world in his palm, much as she had thought she herself had so many years ago. She had been wrong then; she had underestimated her humanness. Was *he* in any way vulnerable?

"Why the frown, princess?" He leaned forward to exclude the maître d', who now worked at uncorking the wine.

Her denial came reflexively. "I'm not—" But he could *see*. And she *was* curious. "I was wondering . . ." The maître d' poured a sip of wine into Ross's glass and waited. Chloe held her thoughts on ice.

Ross lifted the long-stemmed goblet with practiced ease, took the pale liquid into his mouth, patiently let his taste buds warm it, then finally swallowed. "Excellent," he complimented the very pleased maître d'. Without further fanfare the goblets, first Chloe's, then Ross's, were filled.

"You were saying . . . ?" Ross prompted her when they were alone once more.

"I wondered whether you're happy."

"Right now?"

"No—yes, that—but actually more generally. Are you content with your life?"

He shrugged. "For the most part. There are still things I want, though." The directness of his gaze should have tipped her off. She was, however, engrossed in her own thoughts. As she delved further, the softness of her voice spread to her lips, now moist with wine. "What are those things?"

"You hit on them yesterday, actually. I want a wife and children, among other things."

"But you've waited so long—"

"Not by choice."

"Then why?"

His crooked grin did stranger things inside her than even the wine, with its gentle warming touch, was doing. "I guess I'm not *totally* different from the man you knew back in New Orleans. I'm an idealist at heart. I always will be. I have a certain image of what love should be like. If I can't have it that way, I'd rather not have it at all."

Feeling herself suddenly on shaky ground, Chloe looked down. What was love? What would *she* have wanted from it had she allowed it a place in her life? Her gaze caught on Ross's fingers, curling absently around his goblet's stem. At that moment love would have meant reaching out to touch them, to thread her own more slender ones through them. Instead she balled her fist in her lap and welcomed the pinch of her fingernails digging into her palm. It was with disbelief that she heard herself speak again.

"Tell me about that image, Ross. What should love be like in its most ideal form?" For some inexplicable reason she desperately wanted to know.

But the answer was not to come as easily as she might have hoped. Ross stared at her, his eyes a pensive gold. He seemed to weigh and balance, to sift through both sides of a private debate as the quiet sounds of the restaurant drifted by unnoticed.

Chloe waited, sipping wine, feeling buoyed by it. Her own thoughts roamed, though not in debate. She could only admire the divine figure before her, a man every bit as appealing—no, much *more* so—than he had been in her memory all those years. He was a man for today, to be sipped and savored like the wine he poured into her now empty glass.

When he spoke it was on such a potentially jarring note that she was grateful for the wine's mellowing shield. "When was the last time you were home, Chloe?"

"Home?" She frowned. "You mean . . . ?"

"New Orleans. Do you go back there often?"

"No, but . . . what does that have to do with anything?"

"Love. You asked me about it. I'm asking you the same. You loved your family once. Do you still?"

"Of course!"

"But you never see them. Don't you miss them?"

Despite the wine's effect she was quickly on the defensive. "Yes."

"How often do you call home?" he asked gently.

"Oh, every so often."

"And the last time you flew down?"

She hedged. "It was . . . a while ago."

When he leaned forward to pursue his point she saw that his motivation was not spite. He *did* care.

"Why, Chloe? What does love mean to you that you can ignore those same people who worry themselves sick about you? That can't be what love is all about!"

"We're talking about different kinds of love, Ross. One kind you're born into, the other you choose. There's a difference."

He was quick to disagree. "Only at the start. Once a man and a woman have made a commitment to each other and marry, they face those same kinds of triumphs and tragedies that *your* family faced. You've run away—"

"Ross!" Her whisper was hoarse. "Please don't! I don't want to talk about this . . . tonight."

To her relief, though he might have pushed, his tone grew tender. "We've got to talk about it sometime. *You've* got to talk about it. There are so many things you've refused to face, about yourself, about your family—"

"Not tonight," she insisted softly, her face pale, her eyes pleading, despite the dignity in her voice. "I want to enjoy myself tonight. Please?"

Ross stared in utter helplessness, first at her, then at the tablecloth, then at the far wall. When his gaze finally returned she saw a glint of humor. "When you look at me like that, I'd do anything!"

"Anything?" She clutched at humor.

"Anything," he growled in surrender.

"Then . . . tell me about the Picasso exhibit. You *did* see it when it was in New York, didn't you?" She forced a change of subject.

"I did."

"Was it as spectacular as the reviews claimed?"

"Every bit."

She waited for him to say more, but he simply stared at her.

"Come on, Ross. *Tell* me about it."

He hesitated for several seconds longer and his gaze narrowed. "I'm not giving up, Chloe. We'll get back to that other conversation sooner or later. For now I'll humor you."

"I'm waiting . . ." she sang brightly, making light of his threat. "The exhibit . . . ?"

The evening passed more quickly than she could have dreamed. Not only did they discuss Picasso, but they delved into politics, Wall Street, and the National Football League as well. For Chloe, the Châteaubriand Bouquetière with Béarnaise Sauce was incidental, as was the mellow red wine that flowed with the appearance of the beef. Her attention was on Ross and Ross alone.

When was it that she had vowed indifference? That very morning? What a fool she had been to think she could remain indifferent to Ross for long. It was impossible! Her sparkling eyes, her flushed cheeks, her steady smile attested to that. Indifferent? No way! Aside from the physical hold he had on her, she found him to be the most interesting, well-informed, articulate man she had ever known. Though they didn't agree on everything, Ross—as he had promised—respected Chloe's right to her own opinion. It made conversation free and relaxed, neither one fearful of offending the other.

The blend of Ross and the wine put Chloe at ease. When he suggested that they take dessert cheese home to go with fruit, to be eaten overlooking the ocean, she was all for it. Unfortunately, the air had cooled dramatically by the time they emerged from Farmington Court and it began to drizzle on the way back.

"So much for the evening breeze," Ross quipped as he shielded Chloe up the front steps to her door between increasingly large drops of rain. "The living room will have to do."

"That'll be fine. I'm really in the mood for Debussy anyway, and it would have competed with the surf."

Once on the covered porch, Ross smiled down at her. "La Mer?" Was he, too, a music lover, she asked herself? But her mood at that moment was not for La Mer.

"Actually, I had another of his works in mind." The front door opened at Ross's nudge and she went directly to the low shelves by the stereo unit, where she kept a small but cherished collection of the works of the masters. With pride she pulled one album from the lot.

Ross's brow shot up. "L'Après-midi d'un faune?" Again his accent was flawless. "I haven't listened to that in years!"

A spontaneous smile clung to Chloe's lips. "I always called it *Afternoon of a Faun*. I like the way you say it, though. It sounds so much more romantic."

"Hmmm, it *is* a romantic piece, isn't it?"

Was *that* why she had chosen it? Ignoring the note of caution that sounded from somewhere in the back of her mind, she took the record from its sleeve. The entire evening had been romantic; why not this? If she was enjoying herself—and she was—why stop?

Ross squatted to peruse the spines of her other albums. His expression was all male and distinctly wicked when he winked back over his shoulder. "I see you've got Ravel. Should I put that on?"

She had seen the movie, too. "Debussy will be fine," she replied without batting an eyelash, stacking several albums on the turntable. Soon its richly pictorial chords filled the room. Chloe sank into a corner of the sofa, put her head back, and closed her eyes. She was aware of movement within the room, but concentrated on the music floating softly through the air about her. She felt herself in a dream, wakened only by the warm lips that kissed her bare throat once. Her eyes flew open.

"Come sit with me and have some cheese." He took her hand and coaxed her to the floor, where a plate of cheese and fruit sat waiting. Slipping off her high-heeled sandals, she followed his bidding.

A thick cream-hued area rug covered the hardwood floor between the sofa and easy chairs. It was this that cushioned them. Chloe was the keeper apparent of the edibles, slicing fruit and cheese, stacking a piece of one on the other to offer Ross. He lounged casually on one elbow, his legs stretched and crossed as he took care of the wine, keeping their glasses filled.

"You're not trying to get me drunk, are you?" she half teased.

"Are you kidding?" he growled. "What fun would you

be if you were drunk?" Then he hesitated, allowing a resurgence of the wicked glint in his eye. "Are you sure you wouldn't like to listen to Ravel?"

"You don't like Debussy?" she asked innocently, barely stifling a grin of her own. Ross simply topped off her wineglass.

In the hours that followed they talked even more. On impulse, and somewhat shortsightedly, Chloe asked Ross about his childhood, discovering to her delight that he had both a sister and a brother, that he had studied the violin during one of his mother's periodic culture binges, and that he had been expelled from school for a day after tossing a water bomb from a second-story building and soaking the children in the playground.

"A water bomb? Ross, how could you? That's exactly the type of thing the girls always hated!"

"That's why I did it."

"Come on," she chided, her eyes half closed, "a ladies' man like you?"

"Sure. I was eight at the time. It satisfied my need for machismo."

Chloe laughed gaily at the idea of an eight-year-old Ross striving for machismo. He certainly didn't need to strive now; he had it all!

"You have three brothers, don't you?" Ross had picked the perfect time to turn the conversation. She was in a more relaxed, more open mood than earlier. It didn't occur to her not to answer.

"Uh-huh. Allan, Chris, and Tim. They've gone into Daddy's business." Her eyes clouded momentarily. "I haven't seen them in a while."

"Will you be going down for Thanksgiving next month?"

November was the *last* time of year she ever agreed to visit. "No!" she exclaimed forcefully, then lowered her voice. "I think that Tim will be in New York then. I may meet him there. I'm not sure. I haven't heard from him in a while."

"Do you call them?"

"Oh, no, you don't, Ross Stephenson. I'm not so tipsy that I can't see what you're doing. It won't work."

"You won't tell me about *you?*" he asked with such honest disappointment that she almost broke down and yielded. Almost. But not quite. There was too much she didn't want to face tonight. This was a night for the present only. She shook her head in silent insistence.

"Then come here and sit closer." Before she could protest he had shifted so that she leaned against him and he leaned against the sofa in turn. "There." His voice held a hint of huskiness, but she didn't mind. "Are you comfortable?"

"Ummm." She *was* comfortable—extremely so. In fact, there was nowhere that, at that moment, she would have been *more* comfortable. Ross's chest was broad beneath her cheek, his arms were gentle about her, his heart beat a pacifying tattoo into and through her.

Time became an expendable entity; there was no need to move. They sat quietly in one another's arms, lulled by the music that continued to play. Debussy had long since given way to Grieg and Tchaikovsky.

"You and Crystal were identical, weren't you?"

Chloe's answer came before she had time to withhold it. Given the wine, the song, and the man, she felt suddenly mellow. "We were technically identical, but there were always differences *we* could see."

"Were you inseparable as kids?" His breath rustled the hair at her temple.

"Pretty much. Since the boys were so much older than we were, there were only the two of us around the house. Oh, the boys doted on us. But it was different than having a real playmate."

"And you each had a built-in one?"

"Yes. It was fun. She was always the more adventurous. I was the more conservative."

"Yet you were the one who approached me that night, not Crystal. I always wondered why."

Chloe tipped her head back to look more closely at Ross. "We argued about who you were looking at. *I* thought it was me. Crystal claimed you didn't know the difference." She paused. "Who were you looking at, Ross? Was it me . . . or Crystal?"

His lips curved gently, tickling her nose for an instant. "You both looked the same—"

"We did not! Come on, which one was it?" Her teasing was gentle, yet she needed to know.

Ross struck a pensive pose. "Ah, let me think. There was one with dark hair curled to the left, and one with dark hair curled to—"

"Ross!" This time she pinched his ribs, leaving her hand there. "I'm serious! Or were you just interested in any pretty girl?"

Ross sobered instantly. "I wanted *you*, Chloe. I saw the difference. Your sister was just as lovely, but you had something more. I can't quite explain it to this day."

It no longer seemed important to Chloe. Knowing that Ross *had* chosen her was enough to ease part of that guilt she had felt over the years. Ross tightened his arms. "Okay, princess. Now *you* tell *me*. Why was it *you* who came forward?"

"I wanted you more."

When he sharply sucked in his breath Chloe's hand slid lower on his abdomen. Feeling herself on dangerous ground, she raised it to the point where his tie lay in a loose knot, the point to which the top two buttons of his shirt had been released. His chest beckoned temptingly and she allowed her fingertips to explore its warm V.

Ross's voice grew thicker. "You argued?"

"Not exactly."

"If Crystal was the more impulsive of the two, I can't believe she gave up without a fight."

"I wouldn't call it a fight."

"Then what? What finally settled it?"

Chloe held back then, suddenly unsure. "We . . . uh . . . we tossed a coin."

"You did *what*?"

"We tossed a coin."

"To see which one of you would get me?" At her nod he exploded, but a note of humor lay behind his words. "Chloe MacDaniel! I'm appalled! You mean to tell me that you let the toss of a coin decide whether you or your sister would seduce me? That's terrible!"

Chloe leaned closer to his chest, brushing her lips against the man-haired surface as she confessed her crime. "It wasn't a fair toss." Tempted headily by the male tang of his skin, she kissed his chest lightly.

"What did you say?"

"I said"—she gained courage through desire—"that I knew I would win."

Ross held her back, staring in bemusement at her. "Explain, please."

"Crystal and I used to play tricks on one another. We each had our strong points. She always beat me when it came to motivating herself. She was the first to get behind the wheel of the car, the first to choose the prettiest dress in the boutique, the first to snag the telephone caller. I prided myself on being the clever one."

"But what does this have to do with that coin toss?"

Chloe's face held the need for forgiveness. Her voice trembled. "It was my coin. I called heads."

Understanding slowly dawned in Ross's expression, spawning an appreciative grin. "And the coin had two heads?"

"It did."

Whatever he might have thought of her for having cheated, he was undoubtedly pleased that "winning" him had meant so much to her. "That deserves a kiss," he growled, lowering his head. "Come here, princess."

7

~eecceecceec~

Chloe met his lips without hesitation. It was the moment for which she had waited all evening, the moment toward which the night had built from the second she agreed to dress up and dine with him. "Just this once," she had told him then. Now the words echoed through her. *Just this once* she would relax in Ross's arms. *Just this once* she would revel in his love. *Just this once* she would be free of the past. Had it been the wine he had coaxed her to drink that had taken the edge off, permitting her to escape from her self-imposed bonds? Somehow it didn't matter. She was where she wanted to be.

Ross was similarly content, in no rush to disengage himself from Chloe's sweetness. His lips tasted hers again and again, as though finding something new with each sampling. He offered a wine-fresh bouquet of his own in return, a heady brew for them both, warm and moist and intoxicating.

Seeking more of him, her hands spread over his chest,

fingertips awakening to the roughly textured surface beneath the smoothness of his shirt. He was a man of many layers to be explored, one by one. She was the explorer, set off on an ocean of desire, clinging to Ross as to a raft on the rising sea of sensation.

His tongue bid her forward, seeking and caressing hers, sucking her deeper and sparking her instinctive response. She gave it unconditionally, opening to him in delight. Soft sighs were breathed and swallowed, their source unclear. For if Chloe was free of restraint, Ross was no less so. His kiss deepened with urgency, his firm lips holding hers as did the hands that framed her face for his loving.

He finally released her in token protest, his voice a thick rasp. "Do you have *any* idea what you do to me, princess?"

Her answer was just as breathy. "I know what you do to me, Ross. It happens *every* time."

"Does it? I've wondered. Is it *me* or a whole bundle of other factors? It's been a long time since you were with a man."

"By choice, Ross. By choice." Tipping her head back onto the pillow of his shoulder, she studied the strong jaw, the amber eyes, the character-laden crow's-feet, all so very near. "It was never a trial for me before. I've never really wanted another man."

"Is it a trial now?" Even amid their momentarily banked passion Ross was cautious. "What do you want, Chloe? Do you know?"

Her answer was a demonstration. She dipped her head and put her lips against the strong column of his throat, savoring its musky scent. Her fingers were remarkably steady as they tugged at and freed the knot of his tie, then released the front buttons of his shirt. It was her sigh that warmed him when her hands slid over his flesh, but his moan prevented her from going on. His fingers pushed into her hair with a roughness born of need.

"Look at me, Chloe!" His eyes flamed with desire. "Do you know what *I* want?" When she was silent, he continued. "I want to feel you, to taste you, to know every inch of your body. I won't be satisfied with half measures. I couldn't stop eleven years ago—I *won't* stop now. I need you, Chloe. I need to be inside you, to know your warmth around me. Can you accept that?" His gaze flickered over her flushed features. "Will you hate yourself tomorrow?"

She hadn't planned on his questions; it should have been enough that she had invited his lovemaking.

Her eyes filled with the tears of a yearning that was not wholly physical, Chloe moved her lips to within a tentative breath of his cheek. "I don't know what I'll feel tomorrow. I *may* hate myself. But I know what I want now, Ross. I know what I need. I need you. Please . . . ?"

"Why, Chloe? Why now?" he persisted, imprisoning her against his body as he interrogated her. "Eleven years ago it was rebellion—"

"It was not!"

"Then why?" he asked more gently.

She breathed in deeply of the scent of his skin and it gave her strength. "I wanted you. Yes, you were different. Very different. The other men we'd known had been handpicked. Our brothers were every bit as fussy as our parents. But to me you were new. Refreshing."

"A challenge?"

"Perhaps."

"Do I challenge you now? Is that it?"

"Yes, you challenge me. But that's only part of it." The same freedom she'd felt in passion moments before now loosened her tongue, which spilled her thoughts. "I feel drawn to you just as I was eleven years ago. Don't make me try to explain it, because I can't. Lord only knows I didn't want to feel *anything* for you! *You* were the one who showed up uninvited, remember?"

"So you've told me." He smiled dryly. But Chloe was too involved in her catharsis to ponder his meaning.

"And I've told you that you bring back memories to me. Perhaps what I need is to wipe out those memories with new ones. Does that make any sense? Can you make me forget that other time? Can you satisfy the ache I feel with the power of what you are today?"

To her consternation Ross grinned. "You *are* using me!"

With the strength of conviction Chloe pushed herself up to a sitting position, shedding the band of his arms in the process. She was on her own, as she had been all those years. And she knew what she wanted.

"You're damned right I'm using you! I'm using you to show me that I can feel and live. I'm using you to help me put the past to rest. I *need* to do that—I see that now. But don't you see," she ended on a note of pleading, "that you're the *only* one who can help me?"

Silence hung as thickly in the air as the lingering heat of passion. Finally Ross lifted a hand to her cheek. "I want to believe that, Chloe. You have no idea how much I want to believe that."

"Then make love to me," she murmured. "*You* show *me* what love should be like."

He hesitated no longer. With a low animal sound wrenched from the back of his throat, he reached out and pulled her beneath him, lowering his head to kiss her fiercely, to wipe out all that might have come before and leave room only for the present. Chloe put herself into his hands as she forsook all inhibition and returned his kiss with every ounce of her intuitive femininity.

"A tigress unleashed." His lips moved against her neck, then lower, further, to the deep **V** of her neckline.

"I've been wanting to do this all night," he moaned moments before his mouth found the bottommost point of her exposed skin. His hands crept up from her waist to curve beneath the fullness of her breasts, raising them to his lips. Chloe sighed softly, closing her eyes in satisfaction, burying her fingers in his thick thatch of hair to press him ever closer.

With excruciating slowness he eased back the light wool fabric, freeing more and more of her breast to his delight before at last baring its rosy crest. Her insides quivered as his breath tantalized the taut bud and she arched closer. Through the shade of her lashes she saw his tongue bridge the tiny distance to touch the pebbled tip, then circle it.

"Ross!" she cried out in frustration, straining beneath him, needing more. But he was not to be rushed.

"Love is torment, Chloe. It's wanting and wanting and wanting until you would do anything to *get*. Be patient. I'll show you."

Her patience was at a premium. It was tried when he slowly, slowly pulled his shirt from his pants, released the last buttons, and removed it, his eyes never leaving hers. She bit her lower lip to keep from reaching out to touch his skin. He could have been sculpted in clay by Michelangelo. But Ross was real. Human. Warm, manly flesh.

Her patience was pushed even further when Ross drew her up, reached behind to slide her zipper to her waist, then pulled her dress down, easing her arms from their sleeves. Bare to the waist now, she needed his touch. Yet he withheld it, choosing to caress her with his eyes first. Her breasts swelled before him, begging to be cupped and held.

"Do I disappoint you?" she whispered falteringly, driven to ask by the strident ache within. "I was much younger then."

"You're beautiful, princess. You've matured into a

magnificent woman." The edge of tension she heard in his voice was the only sign of his own waning control. "You were young and fresh and eager then. Now you're even better." His hands trembled slightly when he reached out to palm her breasts with such a soft motion that she nearly cried out again. Patience slipped slowly away. When she thought she'd seen the last of it, Ross drew her to him, crushing her breasts against his chest in a move that stole her breath.

"There." He released a low exclamation of temporary satisfaction. His hands moved about her back, covering every inch of its smooth surface. Chloe followed his example, seeking, then exulting in, the steel sinews that begged to be stroked. Eyes closed, she savored the feel of him, letting her fingers play across the broad expanse of his back, then glorying in his chest as he put room between them. His masculine terrain was as rough-textured as her womanly one was smooth. His nipples were as flat and hard as hers were raised and swollen. His neck was as strong as hers was slender. His skin was as tanned as hers was creamy. They were man and woman, so very different from one another. Yet the light in his eyes matched that in hers; it was desire they shared.

Chloe could not have spoken now had Ross demanded it of her. She was awhirl with arousal, every cell coming to life as he touched it, stroked it, put his lips to it. The beat of her heart skipped rapidly on, driving her heated blood through her veins. She was free as she had never been before. Even more so than that night so long ago when her virginity had kept her in temporary bondage, she was free to enjoy the richness of Ross, to relish the fine points of his lovemaking. With desire grew happiness, for she wanted to belong to Ross then more than anything in the world.

Sensing her urgency, Ross took her hand and pulled her to her feet. As she stood her dress slid past her hips to form a pale blue circle on the floor. Holding herself proudly, glorying in the evident admiration in his gaze, she stepped out of it, clad only in the silk panties that hugged her hips.

He held out his arms and she went to them, coiling her own up over his shoulders and around his neck. Breasts upthrust against the warmth of his chest, she burned from within.

"Chloe . . . Chloe . . . Chloe . . ." he chanted softly, reminiscent of that soft September breeze such a short time ago in New Hampshire. But she could not think back; there were only the present and the strong fingers that skimmed the flesh of her hips with such tenderness before moving up her sides and around, as though unable to believe that she was in his arms. She felt cherished, desired, and loved, if only for the night.

"Hurry, Ross." She arched against him, her body aflame with need. "Hurry . . ." This time when he set her back it was to unbuckle his belt and unfasten his pants. His eyes devoured her body hungrily as he shed the last of his clothes, then knelt to remove her panties.

Chloe trembled with excitement as Ross dragged a cushion from the sofa to the floor, then stretched out and held a beckoning hand up to her. But she stood transfixed, unable to take her eyes from his body. It was perfect in every way, thoroughly masculine and fully aroused. Eleven years ago she had been too shy to study him. Now she couldn't help herself. He seemed to stretch forever, with one long limb connected to another by virtue of firmly sinewed twists. Had she been an artist she would have drawn him. Had she been a sculptor she would have molded him. But she was a woman. She would love him.

"Chloe . . . ?"

She took his hand and gracefully lowered herself to lie with him, moaning softly as she stretched against his virile length. He was the source of her satisfaction; she would seek it boldly. Yet there was a timidity in her initial exploration, as though she feared her own power. For Ross reacted to her instantly, catching his breath as her fingers ran along his skin.

"That's it, princess," he whispered in her ear. "I'm all yours to touch." His chest labored in rapid rise and fall. "Go on. Let yourself feel everything you want to feel."

There were two kinds of feeling, the physical and the emotional. Chloe did both. Surging high in anticipation of impending joy, she moved freely over his body. Her fingers found delight at every touch point; her soul found utter satisfaction. She reached his most electric parts as he reached for her. Simultaneously, they exhausted all patience.

"Now, Ross! Now!" she begged, desperate and demanding.

"Kiss me first, princess," he murmured just as thickly. She turned her face up as he moved to cover her, offered her lips as his hips slid between her thighs, then cried into his mouth as he thrust forward to obliterate forever memories that paled in the light of the present.

There was only now. It exploded and flamed like racing wildfire, burning hotter and hotter with the heat of their bodies as it fiercely consumed them. Chloe thought there had never been a moment as complete as that when Ross finally possessed her. Yet the rapture of his surge, within and without, led her onward and upward to dizzying heights of a fiery passion she had not known even that first time. Eleven years had given them both a greater appreciation. Ecstasy's spiraling rise stole her breath as Chloe strained toward that ultimate joy. When at last it came and the conflagration erupted into echoing spasms of heaven, they cried out in unison, then clung tightly, savoring each other's release as fully as their own.

For what seemed a glorious forever, they lay that way.

Finally, his body damp, Ross slid from Chloe to lie beside her. The night air was broken by ragged breathing as slowly, reluctantly, ecstasy eased. Chloe lay stunned in its aftermath. Then, suddenly and inexplicably, she was overcome. Pressing her cheek against Ross's drumming heart, she began to cry.

"What is it, princess?" His voice held his soul.

"Just hold me, Ross. Hold me tight."

He gathered her to him as though she were precious and never to be lost. In his arms, she cried quietly. He understood her inability to explain and simply accepted her need for this further release. His hands stroked comfort along her back, his lips whispered sweet nothings of support against the dark crown of her head.

Gradually her eyes dried and her pulse grew steadier. "I'm sorry. I don't know what came over me."

"How do you feel now?"

"Better." She smiled shyly, rubbing her cheek against the hair-roughened surface of his chest. "Satisfied." She paused, thought. "Actually"—she lifted her eyes to his—"I feel wonderful. That was the most beautiful—" Her words died on her lips as her throat constricted again. Only the luminous light in her eyes completed the thought.

With one lithe turn Ross was on his side facing her. His fingers traced the graceful lines of her cheek and jaw, then fell to run the length of her neck to her collarbone. He laughed at the look of astonishment on Chloe's face.

"Didn't think you could feel it again so soon, hmmm?" He winked with wicked abandon. His leg insinuated itself between hers and she moved against it.

"What's the matter with me, Ross? Have I suddenly grown insatiable?"

"I certainly hope so."

"Ross!"

But his dark features grew more sober even before her

half-teasing admonition. "It *was* beautiful, princess. Even more so than before. I've lived all these years wondering whether I had imagined it. I tried for it over and over. And here, in one shot, you've done it again . . . and more!"

"*We*'ve done it." Her fingers explored his skin, trailing lower and lower, and he gasped.

"*You're* gonna do it again, love!" he growled moments before he kissed her.

This time was slower, more leisurely. Ross was the connoisseur, showing Chloe how to tease and withhold, suffering happily when she did. Chloe took delight in learning the nuances of his masculinity, how to hold and caress him, to lead him to an insanity he never quite reached.

If possible, the force of their passion was even greater, sapping them both with its shuddering fury. There were no tears for Chloe this time. Eyes closed, she nestled against Ross, replete and happy. She had not a care in the world but that Ross should be there when she awoke.

Oblivious to the steady rain that beat down on the roof of the house, they slept. Their closely entwined bodies provided the warmth they needed; the soft rug beneath was their pallet. It was nearly four in the morning when Ross gently woke her up.

"Let's go upstairs," he whispered, kissing her ear in the process.

Groggy and disoriented at first, she reached for his strength. "What-What is it?"

On his knees now, he gathered her into his arms. "Nothing, princess." Yet there was an urgency in his tone. "I want to take you to bed—"

"You're not leaving?" Her arms tightened around his neck in protest. But he chuckled.

"No, no. To the contrary. I want to take you *in* bed—"

"Ross! We've already—"

"Shhh." He grinned smugly. "I want to be able to remember what your bed feels like, for all those long lonely nights ahead." There was an added emphasis as he drawled out the words, as though he half wished she would argue. Having crossed the living room, he took the steps easily, carrying her without effort. "And I want you to be haunted in the same way!" His growl held the ring of truth. "You'll lie in your bed and remember the feel of me until you're ready to burst."

Fully awakened, Chloe felt warmed all over. Her breast was snug against his chest, her hip nestled against the naked stretch of his belly. It was still night; under cover of darkness, she could do *anything*. Her lips turned recklessly to his shoulder, her tongue moistening a spot to make way for her teeth to leave their mark.

"Heeeey! Watch that!" Ross feigned pain as he put her down, letting her slide slowly along the length of him. His hand stayed at the small of her back, pressing her against the solid proof of his need. To Chloe's amazement, her own was nearly as great.

Her lips parted as Ross's descended to draw her into him. There was no limit to this joy, only the demand for more. "The bed," she croaked in haste, tearing herself from him to pull back the quilt and fall onto the sheets. Ross was with her, his body pulsing with the same desire that her quaking limbs proclaimed.

There was a near-violence to their union, a blend of yearning and fear igniting into unbridled greed. It was as if they knew that the end was in sight, as if neither could get enough of the other. Chloe's nails left crescent tracks on Ross's back; his fingers left splayed streaks on her thighs. Neither knew; neither cared. When they collapsed at last against one another, their bodies were slick and exhausted. Again they slept, to be woken this time by the gray light of a morning that was overcast and soggy.

Chloe opened her eyes to find Ross, his dark head

disheveled, staring down at her. Before she could speak he smiled. "I wanted to see if it would work."

"If *what* would work?" she whispered, blinking once, then again.

"I wanted to see if I could wake you up by willing it. I've been lying here just staring at you, concentrating on sending brain waves. It worked!"

"It did not!" she chided. Slowly, slowly, she recalled the night that had finished such a short time ago. "I would have woken up anyway."

"Does your body always feel as . . . well used?" He elaborated with a grimace and a long and undoubtedly exaggerated stretch. But Chloe's mind was diverted.

"Well used? That's one way to say it," she answered distractedly, staring at the ceiling, then rolling onto her side away from Ross.

"Oh, no, you don't!" he exclaimed, hauling her back and imprisoning her with his arms. "After last night you can't turn away from me."

"Can't?"

"Won't!" There had been a wry note of teasing in her voice, but his held none. "Let's get this all out, Chloe," he said gently, releasing her to sit up and face her, an arm on either side of her. Her hair lay in a dark cloud on the pillow. The sheets were bunched around her navel. She could have been a sea nymph, lying bare and natural. It didn't once occur to her to cover herself.

Ross seemed momentarily mesmerized by the image. He looked down at her, touching her features tenderly with his gaze. When he spoke his voice held the intensity of soul-searching.

"I love you, Chloe." She reached impulsively to halt further words, all the while praying that she had not heard the last. Anticipating her protest, he met her hand halfway and pinned it back against the pillow. Leaning down, he kissed her, a long, silencing kiss that echoed his pledge. "I love you. And I want to marry you."

Chloe shook her head as her features grew tense. "No . . ."

"Yes," he insisted more firmly. "I love you. And I'm *going* to marry you."

Her heart ached. This wasn't at all what she had envisioned when she had vowed to spend the night with Ross. *Love?* "You *don't* love me," she argued, totally unable to face the emotional war within her.

"Last night—" he began, only to be interrupted.

"Last night we *made* love. We threw around the term in the physical sense. To say 'I love you' is something completely different."

But Ross knew his own mind. "You can argue as much as you want, Chloe, but nothing you say can change the fact that I love you. I wish I could say that I loved you eleven years ago—it would all sound romantic. I wanted you then. I knew that there was something in you—deep in you—that intrigued me. But I didn't get to know you. A few hours is such a short time."

"It's hardly been much more than that this time," she protested, her voice higher than usual.

"It's been more than two weeks—"

"—during which time we've been together less than two days!"

Ross eyed her in gentle accusation. "Can you tell me that you didn't think of me?"

She recalled her long hours of thought and shook her head. "I can't tell you that. I *did* think of you. But in order to love a person you have to spend time *with* that person."

"No, Chloe. You're clutching at straws now. I love you, and if you would be honest with yourself you'd confess that you love me."

That was what she feared most. There was no place in her life for that kind of love.

"You don't know what I feel, Ross."

"I know what *I* felt last night. And I know that you

couldn't have faked your reactions. Whether you'll admit it or not, you responded to me out of love. That's all there is to it."

"No, Ross." Chloe's response was instinctive. "I'm afraid you're wrong." She knew what she had to say, for his sake and for her own. "I responded to you out of need. Call it lust or physical desire, but don't call it love."

"You're afraid, aren't you?" He came right back, and when he had finished speaking there was a deathly silence. Currents vibrated through the air between them, evoking echoes deep within Chloe. "You're afraid to let go of that past completely. It's become so much a part of you that you're terrified to try to live without it."

"That's not true!" she whispered, her expression forlorn.

"Then why don't you try? You did it for a night—why not for a week? A month? A year? I'm not asking you to renounce your past, Chloe." His tone softened to make way for his own anguish. "I'm asking you to accept it . . . and move on." He paused, suddenly a shade unsure. "You did enjoy last night, didn't you?"

"Oh, yes—" she breathed so quickly that her words stopped dead for lack of follow-up. Ross's smile, a full, warm curve of the firm lips that had given her such pleasure through the night, was enough to fill the gap.

"I thought so." His gaze dropped to her breasts, then her bare middle, in remembrance. When he bent down to place his lips against her navel she clutched his hair. But would she wrench him away or hold him there? The question seemed symbolic of her quandary. As beautiful as the night had been, the morning was dark and dreary. As clear as her emotions had seemed the night before, this morning they were scattered in every direction at once. Turning her face into the pillow, she let her hands slowly slide from his head to the cool sheets.

"I want you to work for me, Chloe."

Ross's seemingly abrupt change of subject startled her. Her eyes shot back to him, gray and confused; her brows knit in puzzlement. "I can't work for you. I have my own business."

"I know." He smiled, tenderly brushing a wayward tendril of hair from her cheek. "What I mean is that I would like to retain your firm."

"For what?" she asked, astonished. It was a twist she had never even considered.

Ross groaned. "To cater our board meetings," he muttered facetiously, then sobered. "Come on, *you* know what you do. I'd like to hire ESE as a geological consultant, starting with a set of revised plans for the Rye Beach Complex."

With the mention of business, Chloe grew self-conscious. Mustering her dignity, she drew the sheet up to her armpits, then sat up. The twitch at the corner of Ross's mouth hinted at his understanding of her mind.

"So it's bribery now?" She forced a feeble smile. "You'd try to hook my business, then slowly reel me in?"

"If necessary." He grinned. Again, though, he sobered quickly. "Actually, I've toyed with the idea all week. It was what I wanted to discuss when I arrived Friday. Well . . . what do you think? Will you do it?"

"No."

"Why not, for heaven's sake? Do you always turn down good business ventures? Really, Chloe, I thought you had better sense than that." There was an edge underlying his humor.

"Actually," Chloe thought aloud, "let me amend my decision. It might be a good idea, but only if Lee handles the work."

"Lee? I don't want Lee! I want you!"

"That's obvious," she drawled, momentarily enjoying having the upper hand. "And that's why I can't work for you." Her sense of conviction emboldened her. "Can you imagine us trying to work together? After last night? I'm not sure how much work we'd get done!" Her eyebrow arched pointedly.

"At least you don't deny *that*," he sighed.

"I've *never* denied that, Ross," she countered immediately. "What I *do* deny is that there's anything deep or long-lasting about it." Even as she spoke she knew her words were a lie. Ross's lovemaking was the deepest communication she'd had with another person in her life. And adding to her dismay was the knowledge that the attraction she felt for Ross would be with her always. There would never be another man for her.

There was sadness in her posture as she slid from the bed, once more oblivious of her nakedness. She paused at the window to muse on how much like the weather she felt. Was this dismal sense of loneliness worth the joy she had felt in Ross's arms the night before? Or was it, as similar tragic moods had been years ago, just punishment for a purely selfish overindulgence?

Ross's footsteps padded softly across the cold wood floor. As he circled her waist and drew her back against him, she sighed. For another minute, no more, she would savor it. Another minute . . .

"I've got to leave this morning."

"This *morning?*"

The warmth of his breath fanned her ear. "Mmmmmm. I've got a date for late this afternoon in New York—"

"Ross!" she protested impulsively. "How can you talk about a date with one woman when you've got another one in your arms?"

His hearty laugh rippled through her. "Ah, Chloe, you are a bundle of contradictions. Warm and soft and sweet"—he nuzzled the hair at the nape of her neck—"but contradictory, nonetheless. You've just refused my offer of marriage—the first one I've ever made, I might add—*and* my offer of employment, yet you're jealous at the thought that I'm taking another woman out!"

"Yes, I am! Unpredictability is a woman's prerogative." She turned in his arms, reveling for these last moments in the manly texture of the skin that rubbed against hers. "Is she pretty?"

In lieu of another laugh there was a glint of mischief in Ross's gaze. "She happens to be my mother!"

"You didn't tell me that your mother lives in New York!"

"She doesn't. She's visiting."

"And you left her for the weekend?"

"With pleasure." He obviously felt no guilt. "My mother has never been the easiest woman to get along with. And the fact that I loaned her my place pleased her more than my company would have. But I *did* promise to take her to an opening at a small art gallery she helps sponsor." He cleared his throat, then spoke with his tongue firmly in cheek. "She's on one of those infamous culture trips of hers."

Chloe couldn't help but grin. "Oh . . . one of *those*—like the violin lessons."

"Like the violin lessons."

Their eyes met in amusement, but it quickly faded. In its place was raw desire, which had returned unbidden and with a vengeance that was in no way eased by the fit of male strength against female splendor.

"Ohhh, Chloe . . ." Ross moaned as he seized her lips.

"No, Ross," she cried, struggling to face the inevitable. "It's too late. We have to—" But her mouth softened at his onslaught and she knew that surrender was imminent. Already the fires of passion had been stoked and her body sought his. Only her mind resisted. "We have to . . . stop. It's not right."

That was all she said. She no longer knew what was

right and what was not. She knew only what she wanted. She wanted Ross.

Ross backed her to the bed and followed her down. She met him willingly. Later, when he had gone, she would face the inevitable soul-searching. For now she played with love.

8

~~~~~~~~~~

Her soul-searching began when the brown BMW pulled from her drive and disappeared from sight. What had he said as he'd kissed her good-bye?

"I'll be in touch, princess."

"No, Ross," she protested, forcing the strangled sounds through a throat tight with emotion. "It's better this way."

He had then sworn angrily, twirled on his heel, and walked away without looking back again. Further good-byes were never spoken.

Rather than easing with time, the sense of loss deepened as the day wore on, forcing Chloe to a deeper level of soul-searching. On this level she found her guilt, and it was multifaceted. First she felt the overwhelming guilt she had expected, guilt that this joy that she had experienced not once, but repeatedly now, should never have been felt by her twin. If it had not been for her original tryst with Ross, Crystal's death might never have been.

It wasn't often that she allowed herself to recall the

details of that tragedy. Now she did. She and Crystal had double-dated that rainy Saturday night and had returned home on a decidedly sour note, which had in large part resulted from Chloe's obvious distraction. When Crystal had confronted her, Chloe had yielded to the ache inside and spilled it all. She hadn't meant to gloat, only to share the glory of her experience with her sister.

But Crystal had been furious. Hurt, jealousy, anger— Chloe had never been able to sort through her twin's emotional rage. For Crystal had run from the house, taken her small sports car, and sped away. Within an hour the police had been at the door to report the accident. After skidding on a wet road, Crystal's car had slammed into a tree. She had died instantly.

As though waking from a nightmare, Chloe twitched. Her forehead was bathed in a cold sweat. Throwing her arm across her eyes, she settled more deeply into the living room chair, awaiting a cessation of the trembling of her limbs. For years she had lived with the guilt that came from feeling in large part responsible for Crystal's death —and for all that her twin had missed in life.

But that was only the first part of the guilt. The second was more immediate. Ross had fallen in love with her and she had allowed it to happen. Now *he* would be hurt and that thought punished her further. It was the last thing she wanted—that he be hurt. He deserved the best, the finest. He deserved a wife and children and all those things that might have been for her, too, had life been different. That she should cause him pain hurt her more than anything in the world. For she loved him—oh, how she loved him!

And *that* was the bottom line, the deepest layer to be unearthed in her soul-search. She was in love with Ross. She hadn't played at love at all this morning. It had been the real thing. Yet it was a hopeless love, a love with no future. There would always be yesterday and the ghosts with which she lived. Ross had indeed stolen her heart, but only that part that had not died with Crystal, that did not die a little more each time she saw the grief on her parents' faces. Ross deserved a wholehearted woman. Perhaps one day he would find her.

Beset with a throbbing migraine, Chloe was in bed by eight to discover the truth of Ross's half-humorous prediction. As he had said, he would be with her then, in mind if not body. The scent of him clung to her sheets, the remembered feel of his body seared her skin. The familiar need burned anew, building to an anticlimax of unfulfillment. Would the torment always be here? Was it a curse he had wished on her for refusing his offer of marriage?

Escape came in the form of sleep. After two nights without it, it was deep and mercifully uninterrupted. She slept as though drugged, awakening only when Lee called loudly from the foot of the stairs.

"Chloe . . . ? Rise and shine!"

Her yawn ended with a sigh of relief as reality flooded back. Life would go on without Ross, much as it had gone on for the past eleven years.

Thus consoled, she climbed from bed, showered, dressed, neatened the upstairs and joined Lee for breakfast.

"Good weekend, kid?" he asked around a mouthful of toast.

"Not bad."

"Well . . . what happened?"

"Nothing."

"He didn't sleep at *my* place Saturday night, Chloe."

"How do you know he stayed over Saturday night? Maybe he went back to New York." With feigned nonchalance, she helped herself to coffee.

"His car was here Sunday morning." Equally as nonchalant, Lee seemed to be amused as well. His was a gentle, brotherly teasing she couldn't resent. Nor would she buckle under to it.

"My, but you're getting snoopy in your old age."

"I live right next door. How could I miss it?"

"You could have looked the other way."

"What? And pass up the pleasure of seeing you blush? You don't do it very often, you know."

With determined steadiness she sipped her coffee. "And I'm not doing it now. What you see is the freshness of morning—"

"—made that much fresher by a stimulating weekend."

"Stimulating," she murmured, half to herself, looking down distractedly. "That's *one* word for it."

"He's a good man, Chloe. I liked him."

"That's funny," she drawled sarcastically. "He liked you, too. The two of you aren't all that different."

"Perhaps because we care about you."

Chloe looked up with a pert smile. "Thanks, pal. I needed that!" Then she dared to change the subject. "When do you leave for Washington?"

"Wait a second, pretty lady. I'm still curious. You and that guy had a thing going once. Is it on again?"

Her voice lowered dangerously. "I never talked about 'a thing' with Ross. I said that I knew him and that whatever might have been between us was over. Don't read something into it that isn't there."

"You make a nice pair—"

"It's not your affair." Her body had tensed in a way Lee had never seen before. Knowing that he had hit a raw nerve, he backed off. Temporarily.

"You're right," he said quietly. "It's not my affair." Then his gaze narrowed. "You know, if I had any sense I'd marry you myself!"

Chloe's outburst was impulsive. "I wouldn't say yes to *you*, either!" The gray of her eyes was hard and stubborn.

"So he *did* ask you." Her partner smiled a trifle smugly. "Fast worker, that one . . ."

Exasperated, she had no suitably indignant retort. Her chair legs scraped back against the wood floor as she stood abruptly, seized her mug, and made to flee to her office.

"What about breakfast?" Lee's voice trailed after her.

"I'm not hungry!"

"You shouldn't work on an empty stomach."

She remembered a similar statement made by Ross on Saturday. "I'll live!" she shouted over her shoulder moments before she closed the door to her office. Oh, they were indeed alike, Ross and Lee, she mused. Was there to be no respite from that dark image that shadowed her?

The telephone jangled, a merciful reminder of the workday ahead. It was Alabama. Had she made a decision on handling the study for the citizens' group in Mobile? She hadn't even thought about it once during the weekend! It would entail a week spent on location taking samples of Gulf water and testing the ocean floor composition. A potentially fascinating project, particularly because the toxic waste burning plan was so new. On an impulse she refused to analyze she accepted the offer.

"Yes, Mrs. Farwell, I'd be pleased to serve as your consultant. Tell me, what is the exact status of the waste burning now?"

A gentle voice responded, its concern undeniable. "The tanker will be leaving Mobile two weeks from tomorrow loaded with oil contaminated with PCBs, which are most definitely cancer-causing. The company that owns the freighter claims that by the time the oil is completely burned, any toxic acid emitted in the smoke will have been neutralized by the seawater. We doubt that."

Chloe made notes as the woman talked. "Where do they plan to do the burning?" she asked.

The woman knew her facts and quickly offered them. The next ten minutes were spent giving a detailed listing of the equipment Chloe would need. She also instructed Chloe to make arrangements with the local university for the use of their lab.

"Terrific," Chloe said. "Then I can make the most of my evenings in analyzing samples I've collected. Four or five days out should do it."

"Oh, Ms. MacDaniel"—the other woman sounded infinitely relieved—"we're so very pleased that you've agreed to help us."

"It's a good cause, Mrs. Farwell. And it's my pleasure."

After she returned the phone to its cradle, a satisfied smile curved Chloe's lips. It *was* her pleasure. Not only was the project exciting, but the escape from Little Compton might be just what she'd need. If—the smile vanished—Ross's image continued to haunt her, she might even have to take stronger measures. At the moment she had no idea what they might be, but she knew that she would not let him sabotage the life she had so carefully built for herself.

Her pencil moved over the paper, making further notes relating to the Alabama project. She would fly down in three weeks, which would allow sufficient time for the tanker to reach its proposed burn site and get to work. Three weeks—that would take her into the second week in November. After a full week in Mobile, Thanksgiving would be at hand.

Thanksgiving. An involuntary shudder passed through her. Should she go home? Alabama was just one state removed from Louisiana; Mobile was only a hop, skip, and jump from New Orleans. It had been so long since she had seen her parents. The void suddenly seemed much greater than usual. Perhaps even one or more of the boys would be there.

But there would also be memories, memories of

another Thanksgiving, not only in Chloe's mind but in those of her parents and brothers. Could she face those? In eleven years she had never made it home for Thanksgiving. They all must have guessed why. Perhaps they were relieved, for to look at Chloe was to see Crystal as well. Was it fair to impose that on a family Thanksgiving?

Her decision was far from made when she turned her attention back to her work, but that course of escape was to be denied her. Once more the telephone rang. "Chloe? Howard Wolschinski here."

"Howard! How's it going?"

"Great! I just got a call from Stephenson." *Oh, no.* "He's ready to talk." *I'll bet.* "Chloe . . . are you still there?"

"I'm here, Howard," she sighed, resigned. She should have known. "That *is* good news." She forced enthusiasm into her voice. "Has he yielded on all of our points?"

"He hasn't yielded on *anything* yet. He simply says that he can see the logic of some of your arguments and that he has no objection to your working with his people to revise the plans." *No objection—hah!*

"Sounds good. My studies and findings are all very clearly outlined in the report I did for you. What I can do is to have one of my assistants—"

"Uh-uh, Chloe. He wants *you*."

"Did he *say* that?"

"Loud and clear. As I recall, his words were, 'If it were anyone else, I'd have doubts. But Chloe MacDaniel has a spirit that can convince the men of the Hansen Corporation that they'd be *dumb* not to follow her advice.'"

"The scoundrel . . ." she murmured under her breath. He'd stolen her own words!

"What was that?" Howard asked.

"Ah, nothing, Howard. Just a thought." Clearing her throat, she made a final stab at escape. "Are you sure he won't settle for another member of the firm?"

The senator's grin was almost audible. "I doubt it." Then he grew more serious. "You will work with him, won't you, Chloe—for me?"

"Howard, how can you do this to me? Why can't you convince him that another member of the firm—even Lee, my partner—would serve the purpose as well?"

"I suppose I could try . . . if I wanted to."

"But you don't."

"No."

"You've just lost my vote." She scowled, though she was not really angry at Howard. It was Ross who seemed bent on disquieting her.

This time Howard's laugh was a full-bodied one. "Thank goodness you don't live up here! With your way with words you'd have the whole district against me. But seriously, we have to get moving on this. The referendum is scheduled for early November. Ross wants to meet with you as soon as possible so that his men can get to work on any changes they agree to."

"As soon as possible—when is that?"

"Yesterday."

I met with him yesterday! "I can't make it before Wednesday, Howard." It was just another job, she told herself. Just another job.

"Wednesday will be fine."

"Should I meet them up at the site?" One place would be as bad as the next. But if there were others with them all the time—and she would *see* to that—the danger of her succumbing to Ross would be lessened.

"Oh, no." Howard quickly dashed her hopes. "He wants you in New York. That's where the drawing boards are. He'll make all the arrangements for your transportation and housing. I have to get back to him later to tell him when. Wednesday, you say?"

She allowed a low but very audibly drawn-out sigh to filter over the line. "It's as good a day as any."

"That's my girl! I'll call you with the details. Okay?"

"You're the boss." After a simple good-bye, she hung up the phone. *Damn him!* It should have been a victory. There would be no need for a referendum and the Rye Beach Complex would be built on an environmentally sound plan. How much better could things be?

An impatient toss of her head sent her mane of hair over her shoulder. With a low oath she grabbed her now empty mug and stomped through the living room into the kitchen, where she poured more coffee and reached for the sticky bun Lee had left for her. It was the open door to his office, just adjacent to hers, that gave her a momentary flicker of hope.

"Lee!" she burst in, rousing her partner from the depths of a thick folder. "Lee, you're just the person I need." So much for gentlemen's agreements; despite what she'd told Howard, if Lee would fill in for her, she'd send *him* to New York. If Ross could be sly, she could, too.

"Umm?"

"I need you to fill in for me in New York on Wednesday. Can you make it?"

Even before she'd finished speaking, Lee shook his head. "Sorry, Chloe. I'll be in Washington." Her face fell. "Why? A problem?"

"No . . . nothing much . . ." Turning away, she mumbled the last.

"Come, now." He sat forward. "I know you better than that. You'd never rush in here asking me to fill in for you if it weren't someth—" The sparkle in his eye grew knowing. "Oh." He cleared his throat as he stifled a grin. "So he called you, too."

She frowned in confusion. "Did Howard call *you?*"

"*Ross* called me. I think his offer is terrific!"

"*Offer? Ross?* What are you talking about?"

It was Lee's turn to be puzzled. "I'm talking about the

phone call I received from Ross Stephenson no more than a half hour ago. He wants to retain our services. What are *you* talking about?"

A furious Chloe leaned on Lee's desk. "I already *refused* him!" she cried, then gritted her teeth. "I'm talking about the phone call from Howard Wolschinski telling me that Ross Stephenson is ready to negotiate changes in the Rye Beach proposal."

"That's great!"

"It's *not!* He wants *me* to work with him and that's the *last* thing I want to do!"

Lee had seen more emotions from Chloe in the matter of two hours than he'd seen in as many years. He was more concerned about her than about either of the projects in question. "Sit down, Chloe." He spoke gently, coming around the desk to enforce his request. She was only too eager to comply, considering the unstable condition of her knees. Lee perched on the corner of the desk, his hands crossed calmly on one thigh. "Now, why don't you tell me about it."

There was a helplessness about her as she looked up at him. "Ross is willing to make the changes, but he refuses to go by my report. He wants *me* to work with his people *in person . . . in New York!*"

"I gather"—he stroked his beard, choosing each word carefully—"that it's not New York per se you object to."

"You gather correctly."

"Chloe, what's the matter?" he asked softly. "The man seems intelligent and honest. You shouldn't have any problem. You can be in and out of New York"—he snapped his fingers—"in no time."

"He thinks he's in love with me, Lee. *That's* the problem. If it were simply a matter of business, I wouldn't worry. But Ross claims that he loves me and wants to marry me."

"So what's the problem?"

"I *can't* marry him." She pleaded for his understanding. "And I'm not sure I can stand his constant pressure."

Lee's voice grew deeper. "What's the matter, Chloe? Are you afraid you just might give in? And anyway, why can't you marry him? You're free."

"Not quite." She touched her fingers to her lips. What if she *were* free . . . ?

"You're not making sense, pretty lady. From what I can see, there's nothing in the world to keep you from marrying Ross."

"What if I don't love him?" she blurted out in a blind attempt to still her friend. It almost worked.

"If you don't love him you're right to hold out. And if you *don't* love him you should have no trouble putting him off for as long as he persists. He'll get tired after a while." Pausing, Lee studied the dismal expression on Chloe's face. "That's not the *real* problem, is it? You *do* love him."

She raised her eyes to the sympathetic ones of her friend and partner, then sought the more neutral tones of the overcast sky beyond the windowpanes. "I suppose I do," she sighed reluctantly. "But I can't marry him. Being with him can only be painful for both of us."

"If *he* believed that, he would never be asking to work with you."

An impulsive "Hmmph!" was pushed through her lips by some unseen force within her. Then her thoughts focused on what Lee had said. "What's this that he spoke to *you* about?"

"He wants to retain ESE as a consultant to the Hansen Corporation. Did you actually say that you *refused* him?"

"Yes. He mentioned the possibility to me before he left yesterday morning." She grew distracted by memories of what had happened after that discussion and wrapped her arms protectively around her middle. Lee's enthusiasm brought her back to the present.

"It's just what we need. You mentioned trying for similar work when we talked on Saturday. The timing couldn't be better!"

She eyed him sharply from behind long black lashes. "Did you say something to him, Lee? You didn't tell him that we were looking for new business, did you?" The last thing she wanted was Ross's pity.

"Certainly not! Don't forget, I didn't get a minute with the man from the time I left here Friday night. *You* monopolized him!"

"Hmmph!" She snorted again. "The man is as sneaky as they come." Despite her refusals, he was obviously far from giving up.

"Now, now, that's no way to talk of the man who loves you."

"Lee, pleeease . . ."

"All right, all right." He held up a hand. "I'll try to keep a hold on that. But let's get back on track. He's offering us an ideal setup. He'll pay us a retainer fee, sort of an advance on services rendered. If we work more, we simply bill him for the overage. If we work less, we still have the retainer. It couldn't be better." Chloe listened as Lee went on. "And the work is right up our alley. The Hansen Corporation is involved in dozens of different projects at any given time. There would be variety and involvement in important issues—"

"You're right, Lee. I can't argue with you." His logic was impeccable. "And by all means accept his proposal —as long as *you* are going to be the one to work with him." The last she uttered with a touch of venom, striking out as she felt herself being pushed further and further into a corner.

"He'd be hiring the firm, Chloe. I might be working on one project, you might be called for the next."

"No! I don't think I could do that on a continuing basis. It would be too painful. *You* can work for him—I won't."

"But your area of expertise is different from mine."

"No, Lee! My mind is made up!"

Surprisingly, there was little tension in the silence that followed Chloe's declaration. Rather, it was as though her outburst had somehow cleared the air. At least, she mused, Lee knew precisely how she felt.

"You know, Chloe, you were right the other day when we talked. I don't know everything about you—all those little secrets you keep bottled up inside. In fact, I didn't even know they existed until this business with Stephenson popped up." There was a comforting quality in his tone; Chloe found herself hoping he might offer some practical advice. "But, Chloe"—his expression grew plaintive—"you've *got* to work out whatever it is that's bothering you. There's something inside you that's inhibiting you. Hell, you should be with Ross right now! He loves you, you love him. Do you have any idea how many marriages are based on far less?"

"I know, Lee," she began, hearing in him the voice of experience, "but a man like Ross deserves much more than I can give him."

"That's absurd!" Lee exclaimed, suddenly exasperated. "If you want Ross you can make it your business to work out those little kinks that hang you up." He turned in disgust, paced to the window, stared blindly out, then turned back. "Damn it, Chloe! You've got so much going for you. Are you going to sit back and let some great mystery from your past ruin your future? My God, I thought you were a *doer!* You wouldn't be where you are today if you didn't believe in working for what you believe in."

Throughout his tirade Chloe sat speechless. Lee had never spoken so vehemently to her. Respecting his opinion as she did, she had to consider the possibility that he was right. *Did* Ross mean enough to her for her to try to vanquish the guilt that had, albeit subconsciously, ruled her life? Could she possibly free herself from the past to give her whole heart to him?

Lee seemed as shocked at his outburst as she had been. His tone softened instantly. "Look, I'm sorry. I came across a little too strong. But I meant what I said. Either you can let it continue to get you down or you can fight it." Frustrated, he thrust the long fingers of one hand through his hair. "Ach, I don't even know what *it* is. But until you convince me otherwise, I have to believe that you can overcome *whatever* it is. Don't let a good thing get away from you."

She smiled sadly. "You just don't understand . . ."

"You're right," he agreed softly. "What say we drop it for a while?" At her nod, he added a final thought. "But promise me that if you want to talk, you'll come to me? I really have very broad shoulders."

Without thinking beyond thanking Lee for his friendship, she stood and hugged him gently. "Thanks, Lee. I appreciate that." Stepping back, she looked up at him, puzzled that, though he was warm and strong and in his way as good-looking as Ross, she felt none of that inner stirring such an embrace with Ross would have sparked.

Sharing her thoughts, Lee held out his hand. "Friends?"

"Friends." She smiled, meeting his hand halfway.

"And we'll accept the offer from Stephenson?"

She yanked her hand quickly back. "No! . . . Yes! . . . Oh, I don't know." She stormed toward her own office, calling out as she went, "Do whatever you want!"

How to go from high to low in one quick second, she mused, settling behind her desk to simmer down. It wasn't easy. If only Ross wouldn't force her hand so! But he seemed determined. What was it he had said about love being wanting and wanting until one would do nearly anything . . . ?

She should have expected something. In hindsight his acceptance of defeat had been too ready.

Now what were her options? She could stand firm,

refusing to have anything to do with Ross. She could send someone to New York in her place for the Rye Beach negotiations. She could also systematically shuttle all retainer work to another member of the firm. It might well be possible to avoid Ross. But did she want that?

Her other option was more dangerous: outward agreement. She could go to New York, both this week and later, with every intention of remaining neutral toward Ross. But did she have a chance in the world of success?

Then, quite unbidden, Lee's words returned with frightening clarity. Did she love Ross enough to fight herself—and her past—for him? Could she go back to New Orleans and face the ghosts, finally put them to rest?

Enough! Her fist hit the desk to evidence her emotional overload. Too much had happened too fast. She simply could not think about it anymore. There was work to be done, particularly if she was to be en route to New York by Wednesday.

With a deep and steadying breath, she sorted through the papers before her. There would be people to call, meetings to set up, reports to plan out before she left. Perhaps the rush was for the best; it would keep her mind well occupied. Worrying was useless. Only time would give her the answers she needed.

Unfortunately, Ross Stephenson was not as patient as she. Yet it was a different Chloe he reached on the phone that afternoon, a Chloe who was strangely subdued. She recognized his voice immediately, had been half expecting to hear it. Its smooth sound sent a brief ripple of excitement through her, but it quickly fell victim to her emotional fatigue.

"How are you, Chloe?" Did she imagine a catch of excitement in his tone?

"I'm fine, Ross."

"It's good to hear your voice. I miss you."

"It's hardly been twenty-four hours since you left," she

chided gently, reluctant to return the compliment. Unwittingly, she had done so anyway.

"You've been counting, have you?"

She ad-libbed quickly. "I'm counting now. I've got five different reports to go through this afternoon, not to mention phone calls, proposals, and what-have-you. It seems I've got this rush job in New York—some snotty executive feels that *his* work is the only thing of importance."

"Hmmm, I can see you got up on the wrong side of the bed this morning." He laughed, ignoring her accusation. "Bad morning?"

"Busy."

"Anything interesting?"

"Uh-huh."

"Ah, we're back to pulling teeth again?" He seemed to be trying hard to humor her. Though her response was civil, it was far from cheerful.

"No. There's just nothing that I feel up to discussing." *With you.* Ross Stephenson had encroached on her life far more than she wanted to admit.

"You sound . . . down." He sounded concerned. "Is something wrong?"

"I'll be fine." She wondered about the truth of that. Where would the anguish end? Much as she fought it, the sound of Ross's voice affected her. She felt tired and drained, yet still able to respond to this distant connection with him. Was his power over her that great?

"What is it, Chloe? Please tell me. Something's bothering you. I can hear it in your voice. Your spirit's gone." He paused, awaiting her response, then blurted out an impulsive "I'm driving up!" before she could begin to offer an answer.

"No! I'm okay, Ross. Really. I just feel tired."

"God, Chloe. You have no idea what *I* feel when I hear that pain in your voice—"

"Then why did you do it?"

The silence was long and heavy. At last, Ross sighed. "So that's it. You've, ah, figured out my messages?"

"You could say that. What I'd like to know is why you had to go behind my back to box me in. Why couldn't you have called me directly?"

When he spoke again there was tension in his voice. "Chloe, I broached the subject of your working for me last weekend. You bluntly refused. Now, I may be many things, but I'm not a glutton for punishment. That seems to be *your* specialty." At Chloe's gasp he went quickly on. "I had no intention of calling you this morning to rehash what I said yesterday. There seemed to be more effective ways of convincing you—"

"—forcing me . . ."

". . . *convincing* you to work with me." He held firm. "It makes good sense. *You're* the one familiar with the Rye Beach proposal and its problems. To bring in someone else would be a waste of time. And as for the other—"

"The other is Lee's affair," she cut in evenly. "He's handling any account with the Hansen Corporation. If you want to work with him, be my guest. I can personally vouch for his credentials and his ability. But *I* won't be involved."

"Then why are you upset? If Lee will be the one to do the dealing, it won't affect you." The resignation he expressed was comparable to the easy defeat he'd accepted that weekend. There was something strangely reminiscent of humor in it.

His argument had sounded so like Lee's that Chloe wondered for a passing moment if the two were in cahoots. "Fat chance," she murmured softly, but not quite softly enough.

"Ah, ah, princess. Let's have none of that. I'd much rather hear soft murmurings about how much you love me."

"Ross . . ." she warned.

"I love *you*."

"So you've said." She tried to sound indifferent, but her tone was more of a plea.

"I mean it. That's why I'm doing all this—"

"What?" she exploded in an unexpectedly facetious show of emotion. "Do you mean to say that you don't value my brilliance, my experience, or my expertise in the field?"

His drawl was devilish. "Depends what field you're referring to. In the field of passion—"

"That's *not* the field I'm talking about and you know it! Why do you twist my words? Why do you enjoy upsetting me, Ross?"

He was suddenly sober. "It's not that I enjoy upsetting you. It's that I want to goad you into facing yourself and your feelings. I love you, Chloe. I want to have you near me. I *need* to have you near me. That's one of the reasons I've manipulated your cooperation. You may not be ready to admit that you need me as much as I need you, but I have no pride. I need you, and I'm not giving you up. Not yet, at any rate."

Chloe listened sadly, torn apart by the anguish she heard in Ross's words. He was being honest about his own feelings. Perhaps he did need her. But, above all else, *she* needed time.

"You're rushing me, Ross. I don't know whether I'm coming or going. Please, give me time?"

His pause was a token one. "You've got till Wednesday. I've made arrangements for you to take the nine-fifty train from Providence—"

"The train? I'd rather drive."

"You will *not* drive!"

"But Ross, it's so much more convenient—"

"—and dangerous. I don't want you driving into the city. Leave your car in Providence. Your ticket will be held there for you and I'll be at the station waiting."

"Ross—"

"It's settled, Chloe!"

Her lips turned down in a grimace he couldn't see. "That's what I like about you. You're so democratic."

He growled a deep "I love you, too," before hanging up.

9

True to his word, Ross met her at the station. She hadn't argued further on the relatively minor matter of transportation. There would surely be bigger battles to fight before she returned home.

As she stepped onto the platform he was beside her quickly, taking her bag and her arm in one smooth gesture. "Did you have a good trip?" he asked, glancing down at her as he guided her through the station.

"It was fine." And she had to admit that there was something very fine about being met like this, something that went beyond the mere convenience of it. Ross's air of protectiveness pleased her—though that was another of those confessions she wasn't ready to make. "Where are we going?" she asked when he hustled her toward a cab, then gave the driver the same Park Avenue address to which she had sent that original check.

It was only as the cab sped off that he smiled. "I thought you might like to see Hansen's corporate headquarters. The team working on the Rye Beach Complex won't be gathered until tomorrow. You might feel more comfortable, though, if you see the layout before you get bogged down in work. I have several things to take care of while we're there."

To her surprise and initial relief, he gave her neither a welcome kiss nor an embrace, even within the more private confines of the cab. Ross seemed all business, as though the teeming life at every turn precluded the leisurely intimacy they had once shared. Chloe was not about to complain; she needed all the time she could get to find her own strength.

The Hansen Corporation was every bit as impressive as she had known it would be. Ross Stephenson wasn't one to do things halfway. As she toured offices that consumed three full floors, no one she saw was idle.

Her guide was one of the vice-presidents, a soft-spoken man whom she liked instantly. Ross himself had disappeared with a soft apology shortly after they'd arrived. She saw nothing of him until late in the afternoon, when he materialized in the drafting room, where she'd been engrossed in an examination of an architect's plans for a museum and theater complex in Des Moines.

"What do you think?"

Her face was alight with spontaneous delight. "I think it looks great, Ross. You have a brilliant architect. From the looks of the plans, this museum will be a drawing card for all of Iowa."

His smile held satisfaction. "That's what we're hoping. Any . . . ah . . . suggestions?"

She grinned. "You mean, will I now go on and pick the thing to bits on the geological score?"

"Mmmm, something like that."

"To be perfectly blunt, I have no way of knowing about this particular project. Looking at the designs, I can mention several potential sources of worry—drain pipes, for instance—but unless I know something about the land there, I can't offer constructive criticism."

When Ross bent to bring his lips nearer her ear, she realized that it was the nearest he'd come to her since she had arrived. She felt the warmth of his skin by her cheek, sending a tingle through her. "Thank God for that!" he offered in a stage whisper, though at the moment they were alone in the room. Ross noticed this fact at the same moment Chloe did. He bent low again, hesitated, then straightened.

"It looks like the day's pretty much over. Why don't we get going?"

Relieved at the steady warmth of his tone, Chloe gathered her things together. It had been an unexpectedly pleasant and interesting afternoon. If each of her days here followed suit, she might make it after all. Yet something hung over her head.

She thought of the days she would spend here in New York, of the time she would have back in Rhode Island before leaving for Alabama, and then . . . later. New Orleans. Should she stop home to see her family? Would it help her work out her feelings toward Ross?

Without a doubt, she loved him. Now, walking beside him down a long corridor, she felt like a true princess. Ross was her prince—handsome, gentle, caring. He loved her. Could she love him enough?

They were both silent during the cab ride to Ross's brownstone. "You'll be staying here," he told her calmly, daring to break the truce that seemed to be in effect.

"Ohhhh, no, Ross Stephenson," she balked, but followed him out of the cab to continue the argument. "I'd like to go to a hotel. This city is full of them. You can go inside and make a few calls to book the room that should have been booked on Monday."

Waving away further argument, Ross led her up the front stairs to the tall oak door, turned the key in the lock, and let them in. Once inside the gracious hall, he restated his case.

"Look, Chloe"—he took her coat and put it down with

her bag—"there are three floors here. I sleep on the second. You can have the third all to yourself if you wish. I'm not suggesting that you *sleep* with me, only that you *stay* with me. It will be more convenient all the way around."

Chloe recalled what he had told her on the phone about needing her near to him. Yet he was suggesting separate bedrooms, on separate floors, no less. Could she really object?

"All right, Ross. You win. I'll take the penthouse."

The grins they exchanged brought back the night in Rye Beach when she had also taken the "penthouse." It was a past they shared; she felt warmed at its remembrance.

"Good! Come on, let me show you around."

This time he *did* do the showing. From first to second to third floor they went, examining furniture, artwork, and memorabilia from his travels. No room in the house would have won a designer's award, yet every room boasted a warmth that reached out to Chloe and made her feel at home.

Ross, too, made her feel at home. He put no pressure on her, so she put none on herself. They ate at a nearby restaurant, then returned for a quiet evening of reading. When Chloe excused herself shortly after eleven, he bid her good night with a noticeable lack of lechery.

"You'll find an extra blanket in the closet, and if you want more towels check the cupboard in the bathroom." He looked up from his papers, though he didn't rise.

"I'll be fine." She smiled. "Good night."

"Good night, Chloe. Sleep well."

One glance back as she left the room told her that his attention had returned to his papers. She took the stairs slowly, first one flight, then the next. This was another side of Ross, one she had never seen. In the past their relationship had always been shaped by the undeniable and awesome physical attraction that existed between them. Now for the first time Ross seemed immune to her charms. Immune? She wondered. Was he immune or simply holding his interest in check? What was his motive? What was going on in that razor-sharp mind of his?

Whatever it was, Chloe was grateful. Living with him, working with him could well have been a nightmare. As it was, she was aware of the fact that he would be sleeping one short flight away. That first night, in particular, she waited, wondered. Would he make the climb? Was his noble intent as strong as it seemed?

The staircase remained quiet, her bedroom door closed. When Chloe fell asleep it was into an insulated oblivion. Ross was nearby to watch over her. The thought left her strangely comforted.

Thursday and Friday whizzed by as though jet-propelled. Chloe's days were spent huddling with the masterminds of the Rye Beach Complex. She found them to be amenable to her suggestions, often mildly questioning, sometimes strongly doubting, but always ready to listen. Ross was surprisingly absent during much of the work, dropping in here and there to check on the progress, but otherwise yielding authority to the men beneath him. When she confronted him Friday evening during dinner, he simply shrugged.

"I suspected that you'd be more comfortable if I kept my distance at the office."

"But aren't you concerned about the project? For all you know the revised plans might be unacceptable to you personally."

"I doubt that," he replied, smiling with silken smooth polish. "I trust you. And I trust the men you're working with. They know what I want." He paused. "So do you."

Her throat grew tight at his deeper implication. It was the first such reference in days, days that had been happy, though busy, for her, and she indulged him the lapse—just as she had let him bribe her to stay in New

York until Sunday with a pair of choice tickets to the Big Apple's newest hit musical.

"How did you ever get seats?" she burst out in excitement, reaching for the telltale envelope. Ross only raised it much higher, out of reach.

"I have ways," he laughed. "You haven't seen it, have you?"

"You know I haven't! It just opened last week and you've known every one of my comings and goings since then. From what I hear the show is sold out for weeks ahead. It's been praised to the hilt by the critics!"

He smiled smugly and changed the subject then, but Chloe easily acclimated herself to a Sunday return to Rhode Island. When Ross announced that he had work to do at the office on Saturday morning, she binged on Fifth Avenue, treating herself to a new dress, shoes, and a purse. Through her enthusiasm, though, ran a thread of doubt. For the outfit was not to be used for several weeks. If she *did* go home for Thanksgiving, she wanted her parents to be proud. If she *did* go home, she wanted to please them. And she could use all the help she could get.

Saturday afternoon was something else. Had she planned a few hours in the city, they could not have been as exciting as the ones Ross led her through. From museum to park to ice cream parlor and back, it was a dream of a time for her. She made no effort to deny, to herself, that she was falling even more deeply in love with Ross. His company was as divine in its spontaneity and intellectual stimulation as his body was in its virility. On the surface, he was holding up well under self-imposed abstinence; only the increasing frequency of the tic in the muscle at his jaw suggested the pressure he felt. She noticed it at the times when they were the closest— standing side by side before a Calder mobile at the Guggenheim, walking hip to hip through the squeeze of the crowd at Rockefeller Center, sitting knee to knee at a small table in a quiet restaurant. Oh, he felt it, too, but that was small consolation for her. Much as his hands-off policy had eased her fears of working with him, it did nothing for the bubble of desire that had begun to grow within her. It was a bubble that grew through all of Saturday, all of Saturday evening, all of Saturday night. By the time they got back in the early hours of Sunday morning it was near to bursting.

After their return from the theater they went to the living room for a gentle nightcap. Their conversation was soft and pleasing, much as the entire four-day stretch had been. Chloe felt that she couldn't be happier. Then she went upstairs, alone, to the bedroom that had been lonely all week. She slept and woke, shifting in bed with little hope of relief from her nagging frustration. She tried to think of anything but Ross—without success. His image, in all its dark and handsome splendor, seemed a permanent fixture in her mind. It was dawn when, after dozing off and on for an eternity of restlessness, she finally crept from bed and walked to the window.

Dawn in the city. Slowly the deep purples and blues of night faded to lighter hues. The tallest of the skyscrapers, visible as she peered toward the east, bore the first pink traces of the ascending sun on its uppermost windows. It was lovely and peaceful; only the dull ache inside her marred it.

She would be leaving for Little Compton today. The thought brought a vivid premonition of emptiness. How she would miss Ross! She had felt his presence acutely during her stay in New York. Even during the times when his own work had occupied him, she had sensed his nearness and savored it. From the first—that night in New Orleans eleven years ago—she had been intensely aware of him. It would be like that always—knowing the instant he stepped into a room, feeling his touch through the air.

As if in proof, she felt his touch now. No sound alerted

her, only instinct. Slowly, but with utter expectancy, she turned from the window to find Ross standing at her door. Standing tall, his features hidden in the shadows, he wore a robe that wrapped at the waist and hung to his knees. From all indications he wore nothing else, and the unruly rumpling of his hair led her to guess that his problem was similar to hers.

The light of dawn passed through the translucent lavender silk of her nightgown, outlining her curves to perfection. Her hair fell in a soft black cascade over her shoulders, offering token protection from a morning chill she was beyond minding. She could feel only her attraction to Ross. Her body cried out for his with shrill intensity, while her mind insisted that she had no right to seek comfort and satisfaction in his arms.

"I couldn't sleep," he said gruffly. "And you?"

Her throat was tight. "The same."

Unable to move, she watched him slowly approach. Each step brought him closer to the window, so that the light illuminated his features. She saw fatigue and frustration; had he been haunted too? Having demonstrated control all week, had he reached the end of his tether?

He came to a halt immediately before her and stood still, looking down. Chloe was overwhelmed and unsure. She wanted him; she didn't. Though his eyes reflected her torment, his hand lifted to caress her cheek with a tenderness that brought tears to her eyes. She couldn't pull away; she needed his love too badly.

Blotting out the sight of her tears, he lowered his head and kissed her. She sensed a reluctance in him, one similar to her own, almost an anger at the force that drove them together. But with that kiss, reason fled. What emerged was a hunger built over days of deprivation, days of temptation and unfulfillment. Chloe helplessly surrendered to its power, mindful only of her desire for complete union with this man she loved.

His hands touched her everywhere, caressing her

through the thin veil of her gown. He found instant satisfaction in her swelling breasts, that filled his palms, and coaxed their sensitive tips to greater heights with the firm touch of his fingertips.

Chloe's movements mirrored his as she thrilled to the strength her own hands found as they wandered across his chest, arms, and torso. His robe was thicker than her gown, and she quickly grew impatient. Her fingers sought his neck and tickled down his chest to open the robe and bare his body to her ministrations.

Ross moaned against her lips, suffering beneath the wildly sensual passage she forged as her fingers crept around his body to glory in his flesh, from the breadth of his shoulders to the narrow slant of his hips. She left a trail of fire along every inch of his taut skin and delighted in his response. Bent on retribution, he inched her gown up over her hips to her waist, then put his hands against her bottom and pressed her against him with a fierceness that brought a cry from her passion-moist lips.

His robe fell to the floor atop the soft cloud of her gown. Then, with his lips drugging her, he lifted her in his arms and carried her the short distance to her bed. The weight of his body settled over her, flattening her against the sheets. For Chloe there was only the pain of wanting him completely. She welcomed his ardor with every pulsing cell in her body, prepared to return the heat of his passion with the flame that whipped through her blood.

"Yes, Ross! Yes!" she cried out unknowingly, clutching at his hips to pull him closer.

But the sound of her voice struck a strident chord and Ross tensed, gasping for breath, with his forehead on the pillow by her ear. She felt him against her, yet he made no move forward.

"I swore I wouldn't do this," he whispered hoarsely, unable to raise his head. "I swore I'd keep my hands off you. I've tried. God only knows, I've tried!" His chest labored roughly against her straining breasts as she lay beneath him, dumbfounded, unable to focus on his words amid her haze of arousal.

When he raised himself to look at her his expression shocked her into sensibility. "No! Don't go!" she cried.

"I have to. For this one release, I'd be buying a huge packet of pain—"

"No, Ross!" Her fingers tightened until her knuckles turned white. She felt close to panic. "No! I need you! Ross . . . I . . . Don't go!"

Again he pulled back, but she followed him from the bed to wrap her arms around his neck. Later she would recall how she had begged and feel ashamed. Now she knew only that she needed him.

"Please, Ross. I've never asked you for anything else. But please . . . now . . . I can't bear it."

The impetus came from her own body—from lips and arms and hips, all working against him. His surrender came in a low moan from his deepest, darkest interior, a cry that spoke of reluctance overpowered. Falling to the bed and rolling to his back, he drew her over him, demanding that she love him for that night, at least, with the strength of conviction. She had been unable to say the words, though she knew they were true; it was up to her body to convey the thought. She had no choice. She was driven by need, by anger, by hunger. But mostly she was driven by love.

By the time the sun's golden rays reached the windowsill and skittered within to glisten across the sweat on their bodies, they lay spent, totally exhausted by the violence of their union. Their rasping breaths broke the air, but there were no other sounds.

There was none of the talk that had characterized their moments after love. There was none of the closeness they'd shared in the past. Rather, there was an ominous tension. For the first time in their lovemaking, their satisfaction was barely skin deep. Even now, it dissipated quickly into the morning air.

After a time and without a word, Ross sprang from the bed, retrieved his robe in passing, and left the room. In the wake of his departure Chloe curled into a tight ball of misery, the covers pulled to her ears. Things were suddenly and ironically so clear. She understood what Ross had meant by greater pain to come; it was the same pain of loss she felt right now. She had seen the agony in his eyes when he had wanted to leave but had been unable to; it was an agony she had shared in the past. She also understood the depth of her love, for in those last moments of panic at the thought of his leaving she had begged for him as she had never begged for anything. And what she had done was wrong. Ross was a man who did things the right way, with no ifs, ands, or buts. He could love her and accept her love in turn only if she gave it freely and completely. The time for play was over.

It was up to her. Everything rested on her shoulders. Ross wanted and needed the totality of her love. If she could not fight her way clear to give it, he would leave her, as he had that morning. For he hadn't returned. She'd heard the front door slam shortly after he left her room. She didn't know where he went, though he returned in time to take her to the train station. Even during the short ride they were strangers, however. It was only as she stepped aboard her train that he offered more than one or two words at a stretch.

"I'd like to follow through with the liaison between Hansen and ESE," he began, "but I think that Lee ought to handle the account. You were right. It will be too difficult any other way—at least for now."

Much as she wanted to argue, Chloe knew that what he said was for the best. The thought of not seeing him sent waves of despair through her. But he deserved more and the force of her love gave her the strength to abide by his decision.

His eyes held defeat when he looked at her a final time

as the train began to roll away. "I'll be here, Chloe. When you're free, you let me know." It was all up to her.

And she was going back to him. Chloe smiled out at the night sky as her plane winged its way from New Orleans to New York. She was going back to Ross.

It was the Saturday after Thanksgiving. The fact that she could easily acknowledge this poignant anniversary was symbolic of the newborn peace she'd found. She recalled her torment, the doubts and second thoughts that had dogged her through her trip to Mobile and the added days she'd spent there wavering, then her trepidation when she arrived at her parents' house in New Orleans on Thanksgiving morning. She'd been distraught, frightened, and unsure. Only the knowledge that Ross loved her had given her the courage to ring the bell.

As the plane began its descent, she shook her head, as much in sorrow for the long years lost as in astonishment that a total misunderstanding had caused such anguish within her family. With a ray of hope, she smiled. She'd call Ross as soon as she landed. She'd surprise him.

As it happened, she was the one who was in for the surprise. Ross himself was at the airport to meet her, standing tall and dark and vibrant. In a moment of déjà vu their eyes met across the crowd. Chloe stopped in awe, knowing that her next steps would be as momentous as those she'd taken toward him so many years ago. But she was a woman now and finally free to love. Breathing deeply, she smiled and ran forward.

Ross met her halfway and crushed her in his arms, holding her tightly enough to eloquently express his love for her. Chloe knew, however, that she owed him more. When she drew back to look up at him, her throat was constricted by the same emotion that brought tears to her eyes. A low "I love you" was the best she could do. It was enough.

His features glowed and she marveled that she could

bring him such happiness. "Let's go home," he whispered hoarsely. With his arm around her shoulder and hers about his waist, they did just that.

A few hours later found them in Ross's living room, sitting on the sofa, facing one another. Ross held her hand tightly as she tried to put into words all that she had discovered during her soul-searching trip home.

"It was a tragic comedy of errors," she began. "I felt so guilty when Crystal died—blaming myself for having upset her, for having gone with you, for having tossed that coin in the first place—that I withdrew into myself. When my parents couldn't get through to me, they sent me to stay with friends in Newport in the hope that the change of scenery would do me good. Unfortunately, I decided that they simply didn't want me around to remind them of what had happened, so I stayed away. It was an endless circle of misunderstandings."

"But it's over?" He sought her reassurance.

Chloe lifted his hand to her cheek, loving its strength, kissing it once before returning it to her lap. "Yes," she breathed. "It's over, though I *was* worried about my mother for a while there. When she learned what I'd thought all these years she was beside herself with grief. We spent that whole first night talking, just the two of us." She paused, then grew more pensive. "I don't think I'd ever had her all to myself before. There were always the *three* of us. Even as upset as she was the other night, she was wonderful. She explained so many things to me. It helped."

Her voice trailed away into silence as she looked again at Ross. His features were warm with understanding, urging her on.

"Mother talked about having twins, about watching them grow, about knowing their similarities and their differences. She pointed out that if the tables had been turned and it had been Crystal who had broken such news to me, *I* would have reacted quite differently. In other words," she went on, with sadness underlying her sense of hope, "Crystal's reaction was part of *her* unique personality, just as, I suppose, the guilt I've allowed myself to live with all these years is part of mine."

"*Is* it?" Ross asked softly, but pointedly.

"It *was*," she corrected herself, looking directly at him. He couldn't miss the pleading in her gaze. "I'd like to put it behind me now. Do you think . . . that is, will you . . . help?"

Her pulse tripped for a minute before Ross's bright smile sent it racing on its way. "That's why I'm here, princess!" he exclaimed triumphantly.

"As a matter of fact," she pondered his words, "why *were* you at the airport? How did you know to be there?"

"Your parents."

"You spoke with them?" That was another surprise. They'd never said a word.

"Uh-huh. Yesterday."

Chloe frowned. "But how did you ever come to call them?"

Before he would answer, Ross shifted her to sit snugly against him. "You were overdue in Little Compton. Lee called me, we plotted your course, and finally put two and two together." His eyes twinkled. "When I heard you'd gone home I knew why. It was all I could do not to join you in New Orleans." Then he hesitated. "But it was something *you* had to do, wasn't it?" When she nodded he caught a strand of silky hair and studied it innocently. "Besides, I knew you'd have to come back up this way eventually. And your parents were more than willing to cooperate."

With her cheeks turning a comely pink, she spoke almost shyly. "I told them about you."

Ross wasn't shy in the least. "Thank goodness for that! It made the explanations much simpler. Say, what exactly did you tell them?'' he asked, tipping his head back and squinting in curiosity.

Chloe basked in his endearing concern. "I told them that you loved me . . . and that I loved you, that you'd asked me to marry you. But I also told them that I had to work things out there with them, to finally accept Crystal's death, if I ever hoped to be as much of a woman as you deserve.''

During her hushed confession all playfulness had drained from Ross's face, leaving a vulnerability that was the flip side of his usual strength. His hand trembled slightly when it cupped her face. "Have I told you how much I love you?'' he whispered, kissing her eyes, nose, and mouth in turn. Her answering whisper came only when he finally released her lips for a breath.

"You'll have forever to tell me, Ross,'' she vowed.

"Then you'll marry me?''

"Uh-huh.''

"Ahhhhh . . .'' With his sigh, he hugged her again. His breath fanned warm against her ear when he spoke. "Tired?''

She savored the manly tang of his neck as she shook her head against it. "Uh-uh.''

"You're sure?'' His arm tightened around her waist. "It was a long flight.''

"Perhaps . . . but I'm not tired.'' Her grin was filled with promise. "I don't think I'll be able to sleep for hours.''

Ross rose from the sofa to cast her a smoldering look. The hand he held out echoed the promise of her grin. "Shall we go to bed?''

Chloe put her hand in his. "That's a great idea,'' she whispered. When he drew her to her feet, it was directly into his embrace. "I love you, Ross. You do know that, don't you?''

"I've known it for a long time. I'm only glad that you can say it at last. You're finally free, aren't you, princess?''

Wrapping his arm around her, he drew her beside him toward the stairs.

She looked up at his dark head, his strong features. Yes, she was finally free, free to love this man forever. "I am," she murmured happily as they climbed the stairs together.

Genuine Silhouette sterling silver bookmark for only $15.95!

What a beautiful way to hold your place in your current romance! This genuine sterling silver bookmark, with the distinctive Silhouette symbol in elegant black, measures 1½″ long and 1″ wide. It makes a beautiful gift for yourself, and for every romantic you know! And, at only $15.95 each, including all postage and handling charges, you'll want to order several now, while supplies last.

Send your name and address with check or money order for $15.95 per bookmark ordered to
**Simon & Schuster Enterprises
120 Brighton Rd., P.O. Box 5020
Clifton, N.J. 07012
Attn: Bookmark**

Bookmarks can be ordered pre-paid only. No charges will be accepted. Please allow 4-6 weeks for delivery.

N.Y. State Residents
Please Add Sales Tax

YOU'LL BE SWEPT AWAY
WITH SILHOUETTE DESIRE

$1.75 each

1 ☐ CORPORATE AFFAIR
James

2 ☐ LOVE'S SILVER WEB
Monet

3 ☐ WISE FOLLY
Clay

4 ☐ KISS AND TELL
Carey

5 ☐ WHEN LAST WE LOVED
Baker

6 ☐ A FRENCHMAN'S KISS
Mallory

7 ☐ NOT EVEN FOR LOVE
St. Claire

8 ☐ MAKE NO PROMISES
Dee

9 ☐ MOMENT IN TIME
Simms

10 ☐ WHENEVER I LOVE YOU
Smith

$1.95 each

11 ☐ VELVET TOUCH
James

12 ☐ THE COWBOY AND THE
LADY   Palmer

13 ☐ COME BACK, MY LOVE
Wallace

14 ☐ BLANKET OF STARS
Valley

15 ☐ SWEET BONDAGE
Vernon

16 ☐ DREAM COME TRUE
Major

19 ☐ LOVER IN PURSUIT
James

20 ☐ KING OF DIAMONDS
Allison

21 ☐ LOVE IN THE CHINA SEA
Baker

22 ☐ BITTERSWEET IN BERN
Durant

23 ☐ CONSTANT STRANGER
Sunshine

24 ☐ SHARED MOMENTS
Baxter

25 ☐ RENAISSANCE MAN
James

26 ☐ SEPTEMBER MORNING
Palmer

27 ☐ ON WINGS OF NIGHT
Conrad

28 ☐ PASSIONATE JOURNEY
Lovan

29 ☐ ENCHANTED DESERT
Michelle

30 ☐ PAST FORGETTING
Lind

31 ☐ RECKLESS PASSION
James

32 ☐ YESTERDAY'S DREAMS
Clay

**LOOK FOR GAMEMASTER
BY STEPHANIE JAMES
AVAILABLE IN JUNE AND
A KISS REMEMBERED BY ERIN ST. CLAIRE
IN JULY.**

SILHOUETTE DESIRE, Department SD/6
1230 Avenue of the Americas
New York, NY 10020

Please send me the books I have checked above. I am enclosing $ _____
(please add 50¢ to cover postage and handling. NYS and NYC residents please add
appropriate sales tax.) Send check or money order—no cash or C.O.D.'s please.
Allow six weeks for delivery.

NAME _____

ADDRESS _____

CITY _____ STATE/ZIP _____

Silhouette Intimate Moments

Coming Soon

Dreams Of Evening by Kristin James

Tonio Cruz was a part of Erica Logan's past and she hated him for betraying her. Then he walked back into her life and Erica's fear of loving him again was nothing compared to her fear that he would discover the one secret link that still bound them together.

Once More With Feeling by Nora Roberts

Raven and Brand—charismatic, temperamental, talented. Their songs had once electrified the world. Now, after a separation of five years, they were to be reunited to create their special music again. The old magic was still there, but would it be enough to mend two broken hearts?

Emeralds In The Dark by Beverly Bird

Courtney Winston's sight was fading, but she didn't need her eyes to know that Joshua Knight was well worth loving. If only her stubborn pride would let her compromise, but she refused to tie any man to her when she knew that someday he would have to be her eyes.

Sweetheart Contract by Pat Wallace

Wynn Carson, trucking company executive, and Duke Bellini, union president, were on opposite sides of the bargaining table. But once they got together in private, they were very much on the same side.

Love, passion and adventure will be yours FREE for 15 days... with Tapestry™ historical romances!

"Long before women could read and write, tapestries were used to record events and stories . . . especially the exploits of courageous knights and their ladies."

And now there's a new kind of tapestry...

In the pages of Tapestry™ romance novels, you'll find love, intrigue, and historical touches that really make the stories come alive!

You'll meet brave Guyon d'Arcy, a Norman knight . . . handsome Comte Andre de Crillon, a Huguenot royalist . . . rugged Branch Taggart, a feuding American rancher . . . and more. And on each journey back in time, you'll experience tender romance and searing passion . . . and learn about the way people lived and loved in earlier times than ours.

We think you'll be so delighted with Tapestry romances, you won't want to miss a single one! We'd like to send you 2 books each month, as soon as they are published, through our Tapestry Home Subscription Service℠ Look them over for 15 days, free. If not delighted, simply return them and owe nothing. But if you enjoy them as much as we think you will, pay the invoice enclosed. There's never any additional charge for this convenient service — we pay all postage and handling costs.

To receive your Tapestry historical romances, fill out the coupon below and mail it to us today. You're on your way to all the love, passion, and adventure of times gone by!

HISTORICAL *Tapestry* ROMANCES

Tapestry™ is a trademark of Simon & Schuster.